By Anthony Ryan

For more information visit: anthonyryan.net

For information check out Anthony's website at: anthonyryan.net

MANY ARE THE DEAD

A RAVEN'S SHADOW NOVELLA

ANTHONY RYAN

Editor: Paul Field
Cover Illustration: Kevin Zamir Goeke
Cover/Interior Design: STK·Kreations

Dedicated with gratitude and respect to
the memory of Marine James Holloway,
42 Commando, Royal Marines.

Per Mare, Per Terram.

CHAPTER ONE

Many are the dead
Who stand in witness
To our crimes.
—*Seordah Poem, Author Unknown*

THE BOY STOOD frozen, eyes wide and wet, his sword hanging limp and useless from his hand as the Lonak warrior came for him. The lad's bleached features lacked any real expression, as if the impending certainty of his own death had somehow slipped beneath his notice. Sollis had seen this many times before, the face of one experiencing their first taste of real battle.

The charging Lonak and his hapless prey were a good dozen

yards away. The warrior was wounded, one of Brother Smentil's arrows jutting from the tattooed flesh of his right arm. The limb flailed like a rag as he closed on the young Realm Guard, using his good arm to raise his war club high. It was a difficult distance for a knife throw, but Sollis had exhausted his arrows during the first few minutes of the skirmish.

The small, triangular bladed knife spun as it left his hand, describing a deceptively lazy arc through the air before sinking into the back of the Lonak's neck. Sollis grunted in frustration as he saw that the knife had missed the man's spine by a clear inch. Nevertheless, his charge came to an abrupt end as the knife struck home. He staggered, war club still raised as he tottered barely a yard from the frozen boy-soldier.

"Kill him!" Sollis shouted. The youth, however, seemed deaf to the call, continuing to stare with moist but empty eyes at the shuddering man before him. Sollis started forward then halted at the sound of feet scraping loose rock.

He sank to a crouch, spinning as he did so, the Order blade flickering across the wolf-pelt-covered torso of another Lonak. The man's war club whistled over Sollis's head as the star-silver edged steel cut through fur and the flesh beneath. The Lonak reeled back, sliced open from belly to shoulder, a shout of fury and pain erupting from his mouth. The wound was plainly mortal but, as was usual with his kind, the Lonak refused to surrender to death whilst there was still a chance to kill the hated Merim Her. Blood streamed from the Lonak's mouth as he sang, drawing back his club for another blow. Although the words were garbled, Sollis possessed sufficient understanding of his language to discern the cadence of a death-song.

Seeing another Lonak beyond the dying warrior's shoulder, Sollis flicked his sword across the man's throat and stepped to the side to avoid the spear thrust of his charging comrade. It was a good thrust, straight, swift and true, missing Sollis's chest by bare inches as he twisted, sword extended to skewer the second Lonak through the eye. This one was a woman, tall and lean, head shaven but for the long scalp-lock that sprouted from the base of her skull. She had no chance to give voice to the song that would carry her into the gods' embrace. Death came the instant the sword point reached her brain, although she hung on the blade twitching for a time until Sollis withdrew it.

The two Lonak collapsed against each other, forming a strange pyramidal tableau as they sank to the rocky ground, heads resting on the shoulder of the other, almost like lovers sharing a last intimate moment before slumber.

Sollis blinked and turned away, intending to resume his charge towards the boy-soldier and his assailant, expecting to find the lad lying on the slope with his head bashed in. Instead, he stood over the body of his erstwhile attacker, grunting as he tried in vain to tug his sword free of the Lonak's ribcage. His face was more animated now, colour returning to the pale immobile mask and tears streaking his cheeks. Apart from the boy's grunts a familiar post-battle quiet had descended on the canyon.

Glancing around Sollis saw his brothers descending the western slope. There were sixty besides himself, less than half the number of the war band they had just despatched, but the shock of their attack had done much to even the odds. Distracted by their slaughter of the Realm Guard, the Lonak had neglected to guard their rear.

As they descended into the canyon the brothers paused to finish off those Lonak who had not yet succumbed to their wounds. It was a long-ingrained tradition of the Sixth Order not to show mercy to these people, as the only reward was a knife in the back as soon as they recovered sufficiently to attempt an escape. A few Realm Guard survivors stood around clutching wounds or staring in shock at the remnants of their regiment. Over three hundred cavalry had trooped into this narrow canyon just a quarter-hour before. Sollis reckoned less than a third still lived. Most of their horses had survived the ambush, however; the Lonak were always keen to get their hands on Realm-bred stock.

"You," he said, advancing towards the boy who was still engaged in a struggle to free his sword from the fallen warrior. "Who's in charge of this farce?"

The young Realm Guard gaped at him in blank incomprehension, causing Sollis to wonder if his mind might have been unhinged by the recent carnage. Then the boy blinked and raised a hand from his sword hilt, pointing a finger at the base of the canyon. Sollis felt a small pulse of admiration for the way the youth managed keep the tremble from his hand.

"There, sir," he said, his voice coloured by the burr of those raised on the south Asraelin shore. He was a long way from home. "Lord Marshal Al Septa."

"I'm a brother not a sir," Sollis corrected, following the boy's finger to a pile of bodies in the centre of the canyon. At least a dozen Realm Guard had fallen there, covered by a small forest of the hawk-fletched arrows favoured by the Lonak. The pile of corpses twitched slightly but Sollis's experienced eye told him none of these men still held on to life.

"Spared himself the disgrace of a trial before the king, at least," he muttered. "This mad jaunt north of the pass was his idea, I suppose?"

"The Wolf Men destroyed three villages before fleeing back to the mountains," the boy said, a defensive note colouring his tone. "Killing all the folk they could find, and they weren't quick about it. Lord Al Septa was driven by a desire for justice. He was a good man."

"Well." Sollis pushed the boy aside and took hold of his sword. "All he managed to do was drive most of you to an early communion with the Departed. Good men can be fools too." He gripped the sword with both hands, putting his boot on the dead man's chest as he dragged the blade clear. A wet sucking sound rose as it came free, followed by a brief fountain of blood and a nostril stinging stench as the man's lungs let go of his last breath.

"Always better to go for the belly or the throat, if you can," Sollis said, returning the sword to the boy. "Less chance of it getting stuck."

"Faith! How old are you, lad?"

Sollis turned to find Brother Oskin approaching, his weathered features drawn into a squint as he surveyed the boy-soldier. Red Ears, his ever present Cumbraelin hunting hound, trotted from his side to snuffle at the Lonak corpse, her long tongue flicking out to lap at the blood leaking from its wound. Oskin allowed the beast a few more licks before nudging her away with a jab of his boot. It had been thanks to Red Ears' nose that they tracked the Lonak war band, so it would have been churlish to deny her a small reward, although Sollis wished the beast had managed to find them soon enough to prevent this massacre.

"Fourteen," the boy replied, casting a nervous glance at the massive hound as Red Ears sauntered towards him, licking the blood from her chops. "I'll be fifteen in a month."

"The king sends children to fight the Lonak," Oskin said with a despairing shake of his head. "Your mother know where you are?"

A certain hardness crept into the lad's gaze as he replied in a low mutter, "No. She's dead."

Oskin gave a soft sigh before turning back to Sollis. "Smentil took a shaman alive, thought you might want to talk to him. Best be quick if you do, I doubt he'll last long."

Sollis nodded and moved off, issuing orders over his shoulder as he climbed the far slope of the canyon. "Get these horses rounded up. See if there's anything to be done for the Realm Guard wounded, and see if you can find one with any kind of rank. This lot will need a captain for the journey south."

"That I will, brother." Oskin clapped a hand on the boy's shoulder and guided him to the canyon floor where most of the Realm Guard had begun to gather. "Come on, whelp. You can point me to a sergeant, if there's any left."

"It's Jehrid," the boy said in a sullen mutter as Oskin led him away.

Sollis found Brother Smentil standing over the slumped and bleeding form of a wiry Lonak of middling years. His status as shaman was proclaimed by the swirling tattoo covering his shaven skull. The exact meanings of the various symbols with which the Lonak covered themselves were still beyond Sollis's understanding, but he knew enough to distinguish the signs of a warrior or a hunter from that of a shaman.

Gut wound, Smentil told Sollis, his hands making the signs with a flowing precision that came from years of necessary practice. The tall brother held the unenviable distinction of being the only member of the Sixth Order to be captured by the Lonak and survive the experience, albeit losing his tongue in the process. Consequently, the Order's sign-language was his primary means of communication apart from the occasional written note in a near illegible script.

Sollis angled his head as he surveyed the dying shaman, finding himself confronted by a typically hate-filled glare. He spoke as he locked eyes with Sollis, bloody spittle spilling from his lips and staining his teeth as he formed the words. "*Merim Her, fogasht ehl mentah. Shiv illahk tro dohimish.*" *Merim Her, always there are more. Like maggots on a corpse.*

"*Ver dohimishin,*" Sollis replied: *You're dying.* He sank to his haunches, speaking on in Lonak, "Do you wish a quick death?"

The shaman snarled, face quivering with the effort of meeting Sollis's gaze. "I want nothing from you."

"No raids for nearly a year," Sollis went on. "Now you lead a war band of many spears to our lands. You steal nothing, take no treasure or captives. All you do is burn and kill. Why?"

A suspicious glint crept into the shaman's eye as he narrowed his gaze. "You know why… blue-cloak," he said in a hard, pain-filled rasp.

"No," Sollis assured him with a humourless smile. "I don't.

Tell me." He held the shaman's gaze, seeing no sign he might yield. Sollis was tempted to draw his dagger and start probing the man's wound, though past experience told him the Lonak were too inured to pain for such encouragement to bear fruit.

"I can take you with us," he said instead. "Back to the Pass. We have healers there. Once you are made whole I will put you in a cage and parade you through the lands you raided. Merim Her will spit upon you, cast their filth at you, and no Lonak will ever hear your story again."

The shaman's nostrils flared as he drew in a series of rapid breaths. Blood began to seep through the fingers the man had clamped over his wound and Sollis saw his eyes take on a familiar, unfocused cast. "No, blue-cloak," the shaman said, a crimson torrent now flowing from his mouth as he grinned at Sollis, speaking in harsh grunts. "I... am being called... to the Gods' embrace... where my story will live forever... in their ears."

"Tell me!" Sollis reached out to clamp a hand on the shaman's neck, gripping hard. "Why did you raid?"

"You... Because of you..." The shaman's grin broadened, allowing a slick of blood to cover Sollis's hand. "You came into the mountains... and brought that which is known only to the Mahlessa... She decreed... vengeance..."

The shaman's eyes dimmed and closed, his head lolling forward as Sollis felt his final pulse, no more than the faintest flutter against his palm.

What did he mean? Smentil's hands asked as Sollis rose, hefting his canteen to wash away the blood. Like most of the brothers Smentil had only a partial understanding of Lonak. Sollis, by contrast, had used his years at the Pass to learn as much as he could. It had been a tortuous business, reliant on rarely taken captives and the few relevant books he had gleaned from the Third Order library. Whilst Lonak prisoners almost never divulged information of any value, they were always enthusiastic in assailing their captors with all the insults they could muster, which added greatly to his vocabulary and understanding of syntax. It also meant he spoke a version of Lonak even harsher than the original.

"*Rova kha ertah Mahlessa,*" he said, flicking the pinkish water away and turning his gaze north. The sun was well past its zenith and the shadows grew long on the mountains. High on the granite slopes the stiffening wind swept snow into a clear blue sky. As always when he gazed upon these peaks there was the sense of his scrutiny being returned. Bare as they seemed, the chances of journeying through the Lonak dominion unobserved were always slender at best. Veteran brothers had a saying, 'The mountains have eyes.' *She'll learn of what happened here within days*, he thought. *What will she do then?*

"'That which is known only to the Mahlessa,'" he elaborated, turning back to Smentil. "The Dark, brother. He was talking about the Dark."

He made for the crest of the slope and began to descend to where they had tethered their horses. "Best get these guardsmen into some semblance of order," he said. "We're returning to the Pass with all speed. The Brother Commander must know of this."

TWO

I T TOOK A night and a day to reach the Skellan Pass. Sollis pushed his mingled company hard, maintaining a punishing pace and refusing to rest come nightfall despite the condition of the wounded Realm Guard, three of whom expired before the journey was done. He had expected some level of condemnation from their fellow guardsmen but they remained a mostly silent lot. Throughout the journey their eyes continually roved the peaks and valleys in wary trepidation, faces pale with a fear that wouldn't fade until they were far from these lands.

"They were like ghosts," Jehrid, the boy-soldier, said in response to Brother Oskin's request for an account of his regiment's demise. "Just seemed to spring out of the air. The lads think it was some Dark spell cast by their shaman."

"Dark spell, eh?" Oskin enquired with an amused snort.

"How else to explain it?" Jehrid replied, face reddening a little. "Two hundred men just appearing out of nowhere. And the way they fought..." He grimaced and shook his head. "Not natural."

"One hundred and eighteen," Sollis said. He didn't bother to turn as he steered his mount along the ridgeline which descended in a gradual slope to the sparsely grassed plain north of the Pass. "And they weren't all men. The Lonak don't need the Dark to ambush fools, boy. This is their land and they know every stone of it."

The narrow gate in the Pass's northernmost wall trundled open after the customary delay as the sentries on the parapet ensured the approaching party were not Lonak in disguise. It was a ruse their enemy hadn't attempted in decades, but the Order never forgot a hard lesson. Sollis led the company inside to wind their way through the twists and turns of the inner fortifications until they emerged into the courtyard.

"Get the wounded to the healing house," Sollis told Oskin, climbing down from the saddle. "And find room for the rest to bed down. I'll report to the Brother Commander."

After stabling his horse he made his way to the tallest of the towers which crowded the southern stretch of the Pass. "He's got company," Brother Artin advised as Sollis strode through the door. He and Sollis were the most senior brothers stationed at the Pass. Artin had responsibility for the day-to-day running of the garrison whilst Sollis oversaw forays beyond the fortifications. He felt no resentment at the disparity in their roles. Artin was a sound leader and no slouch in combat, but his stolid attachment to routine made him a better fit for commanding a fortress. Sollis, by contrast, would sometimes contrive excuses to patrol north of the Pass if he spent more than a few days within these walls.

"Urgent business, brother," he told Artin, not pausing in his stride. "Something you should hear too," he added before knocking on the door to the Brother Commander's chamber with a forcefulness he hoped fell short of causing offence. There was a brief interval before he heard a muffled, "Come in," in a tone he was relieved to find free of irritation.

"Brother Sollis." Brother Commander Arlyn sat behind his desk, greeting him with his customary faint smile, one eyebrow raised in curiosity. "Back early, I see."

"With intelligence, brother," Sollis said, his gaze immediately drawn to the room's other occupant. She sat in a chair before Brother Arlyn's desk, blonde hair shifting as she turned to regard Sollis with an open smile and inquisitive blue eyes. Apart from the occasional Lonak captive, women were a decided rarity at the Pass, though he had a sense that a woman like this would be a rarity anywhere.

"Do you know Sister Elera?" Arlyn enquired. "She arrived this morning. Come all the way from Varinshold on a mission of some import."

Sollis, realising he was staring, took note of the woman's grey robe before shifting his gaze. "I do not, brother," he said. "I bid you welcome, sister. We can always use another healer. In fact, presently there are Realm Guard requiring assistance in the courtyard."

"In a moment, sister," Arlyn said as Elera began to rise. "If they've lasted this long, I daresay they can last a little longer. Our own healers know their business in any case." His eyes took on a more serious cast as he turned back to Sollis. "You found the war band, I take it?"

"We did, brother," Sollis confirmed. "Came upon them in the midst of slaughtering a regiment of Realm Guard cavalry. Apparently, their Lord Marshal thought pursuing the Lonak into their own dominion little different from chasing after a gang of common outlaws."

"I don't envy his interview with the king," Artin commented from the doorway.

"He's dead," Sollis told him. "Fortune was merciful." He saw Sister Elera's smooth brow crease in a frown of disapproval and felt compelled to elaborate. "The king is not renowned for his indulgence of incompetence, sister."

"No," she conceded with a small shrug. Her voice was smooth and cultured, lacking any trace of the streets or the fields. "But the Faith teaches that judgment should be left to the Departed."

"Our casualties?" Brother Arlyn asked.

"None," Sollis told him. "Though Brother Hestin is complaining of a sprained wrist. We brought back ninety Realm Guard, including wounded."

"A grim toll," Arlyn observed. "But the mission can still be counted a success."

"There's something else, brother." Sollis paused to cast a wary glance at Sister Elera.

"Speak freely," Arlyn said. "As I said, our sister is here on a particular mission and I suspect your intelligence will enlighten her as to its wisdom."

"There was a Lonak shaman amongst the war band." Sollis looked over his shoulder and gestured for Artin to close the door, waiting until he had done so before continuing. "He lived long enough to tell us the raid was ordered by the Mahlessa in retribution for something we had done. He made mention of the Dark before he died."

"Mahlessa?" Sister Elera asked.

"The High Priestess of the Lonak," Arlyn explained. "The clans feud amongst each other constantly, but they all answer when the Mahlessa calls." His eyes settled on Sollis. "Whatever their faults as a people, the Lonak are even less prone to superstition than the Faithful, despite their attachment to god-worship."

"Indeed, brother," Sollis agreed. "For a shaman to make mention of it would indicate trouble in the mountains. Trouble the Mahlessa, for whatever reason, has blamed on the Order."

Arlyn pursed his lips and turned to Elera. "So you see, sister. This would appear to be a particularly ill-chosen moment to pursue your course."

Elera gave a brisk smile in response, nodding at the opened letter on Arlyn's desk. "Nevertheless, the Aspects of all six orders have chosen it. It is not for us to gainsay their authority, merely to fulfil their instructions."

Sollis saw Arlyn smother a sigh as he gestured him forward, pointing at the letter. "I think your counsel would be welcome here, brother."

Sollis duly retrieved the single page of parchment, reading it through quickly. It was set down in neat precise letters, presumably the work of a Third Order scribe, and signed by all six Aspects of the Faith. He took particular note of the fact that Aspect Andril, the aged but highly respected head of the Sixth Order, had seen fit to underline his signature, twice.

"You wish to travel into the mountains," Sollis said to Elera, frowning as he read through the letter's final paragraph. "In search of this... weed?"

"Quite so, brother," she responded, her brisk smile still in place. She reached into a pocket in her robe and extracted a small paper scroll, unfurling it to reveal a drawing. It depicted what appeared to Sollis to be an unremarkable plant, a cluster of narrow stems from which sprouted small four-petalled flowers. "Jaden's Weed, to be precise," she said. "Perhaps you've encountered it during one of your many daring northward quests."

Sollis's frown deepened at that and he saw her mouth twitch a little. "I've no memory of it," he said, glancing at the drawing again and shaking his head.

"My research indicates it can be found in a particular place," Elera said, furling the scroll. "Morvil's Reach. Do you know of it?"

Brother Artin gave a derisive snort. "Morvil's Folly we call it, sister," he said. "You want to go there?"

"It seems the best place to start," she replied, apparently unconcerned by his half-amused, half-appalled tone. "Does this present a particular difficulty?"

"Oh, not at all." Artin raised his eyebrows in mock

solicitation. "Once you discount the fact that it's a good sixty miles into the mountains and smack in the middle of the lands held by the Grey Hawk Clan, the most numerous and warlike clan in the Lonak Dominion, I'd say it presents no difficulty at all."

"Brother." Arlyn spoke softly, but the single word was enough for Artin to fall silent. He crossed his arms and retreated to a corner, heavy brows bunched in disapproval.

"Brothers," Elera said, her smile now replaced by something more genuine and open. "Please do not think I am ignorant of the risks involved. I would not undertake them, nor ask others to do so, unless the matter was not both urgent and necessary."

"As the Aspects' letter states," Arlyn said. "And yet the reason for such urgency is not explained."

Elera lowered her gaze, all trace of humour leaving her features. "No word of what I am about to say is to leave this room," she said, lifting her head to regard each of them in turn, eyes hard with sincere gravity. "I require your word as servants of the Faith."

"You have it," Arlyn said. After Sollis and Artin had also voiced their assurance Elera nodded.

"Four weeks ago," she began, "a ship from the far off Volarian port of Vehrel docked in Maelinscove. Half the crew were found to be dead and most of the others stricken by sickness. Their symptoms…" She trailed off, taking a deep breath before continuing. "Their symptoms were consistent with the disease we know as the Red Hand."

She fell silent, letting the words settle. Brothers of the Sixth Order were not prone to overt expressions of emotion but even so Artin couldn't contain a soft and rarely heard obscenity whilst the Brother Commander merely closed his eyes, Sollis noticing how his long fingered hands twitched briefly before he clasped them together. His own reaction was internal, a rush of memory, mostly unwelcome and not often dwelt upon. The livid red marks that encircled his mother's neck, the tears that always rose in her eyes whenever she spoke of those terrible days. She had been only an infant when the Red Hand swept through the four fiefs. There had been no Realm then, King Janus himself just a callow youth who barely survived his own brush with the plague. In those days the four fiefs bickered and warred constantly, endless columns of soldiers trampling the crops that surrounded the border hamlet where his mother lived. Then one day they stopped.

Dead men can't march, she told him decades later. *We found hundreds littering the fields, thousands even. Your grammy and I went out to rob the dead, as was custom. Don't you look at me like that, boy! Lords and their wars do nothing but take food from the mouths of folk like us. Only fair we take something back when we can. 'Cept this time we took something best left behind.*

She went on to tell him how the hamlet had died. A poor but mostly peaceful community that had persisted in the borderlands between Asrael and Cumbrael for nigh on a century, wiped out in the course of a few days. Sollis's mother woke from her fever to find herself staring into his grandmother's empty eyes. *By the time it was over the only ones left were me, Fram the wheelwright and the gormless loon they called the pig-boy. Still, we'd just gathered the harvest so there was plenty to go around that winter.* She had laughed then, as was her wont when voicing dark humour. She rarely laughed otherwise, but then Sollis recalled her having little to laugh about.

"So it's come back," he said to Elera. "How far has it spread?"

"Fortunately, the outbreak was swiftly contained," she said. "One of King Janus's earliest acts on ascending the throne was to institute a strict protocol for dealing with any vessel found to be carrying the Red Hand. The ship was towed far out to sea and fire arrows used to burn it."

"Along with its crew, I presume?" Arlyn enquired. "Even those who had not yet succumbed."

"The King's Word may be harsh at times," she replied. "But often it has saved us from disaster, as in this case. There was a fair amount of panic in the port, of course. So the king arranged for certain rumours to be spread attributing the ship's demise to poisoning or some god-worshipper's Dark design. More concerning was the news imparted by one of the crew before he expired. It seems the Red Hand now has a firm hold in Vehrel, a port from which merchant vessels sail to all corners of the world."

"Then," Sollis said, "it's only a matter of time before another plague ship turns up at our door."

"I fear so, brother."

He nodded at the scroll in her hand. "And this weed of yours?"

"The Fifth Order has spent decades trying to develop a curative for the Red Hand, without any real success. With the advent of the current crisis I was charged by my Aspect to review all the historical accounts held by our Order. It was hoped that I might find something others had missed." She looked at the scroll, giving a tight smile. "I found this. There is a fragmentary account of a Renfaelin campaign against the Lonak. A century ago an army of knights advanced into the mountains…"

"And never marched out again," Artin said. "We know the story, sister. They were led by Baron Valeric Morvil, said to be the greatest knight of his age. It was him who built the folly now named in his honour." He shook his head in professional disdain. "Only a Renfaelin noble would think to build a castle in the mountains. I'm sure the Lonak must have found it all very amusing. The story goes they actually let him finish it before wiping out his entire command in a single night."

"That campaign was accompanied by a brother from the Third Order," Elera said. "He sent periodic reports back to Varinshold, which stopped eventually for obvious reasons. However, the final account speaks of a captured Lonak shaman using this weed to cure a knight named Jaden, a knight whose symptoms indicate he may have contracted a variant of the Red Hand."

"Variant?" Sollis asked. "There's more than one kind?"

"Diseases change over time, brother," she explained. "They grow, become more contagious, more virulent. It's what made the plague so damaging when it swept through the four fiefs. We had never encountered its like before, so had no means of fighting it. The account relates how this weed," she held up the scroll once more, "was found in close proximity to Morvil's outpost. If we can find it, we may have a chance of stopping the Red Hand should it return."

"A chance to commit suicide, more like," Artin said, holding up a hand at her scowling response. "I'm sorry, sister, but this is…"

"Our mission," Brother Commander Arlyn broke in. "As ordained by the Aspects of the Faith," he added, meeting Sollis's eyes. "Tell me truly, brother, can you get to Morvil's Reach and return safely?"

"Perhaps," Sollis said. "With a small group. No more than four. But if the Mahlessa has raised the Lonak against us…"

"Then it's possible you might also discover the cause of this current unrest." The perennially faint smile returned to Arlyn's lips. "Two bucks with one arrow. Choose your brothers and be ready to leave by morning."

"YOU KNOW THIS is a hopeless mission," Artin whispered as he and Sollis stepped out into the corridor.

"And yet hope remains the heart of the Faith, brother," Sollis replied, earning a scowl in response before Artin strode off, shoulders hunched in anger. Sollis, hearing Arlyn's voice, paused for a second, glancing back to see Sister Elera in the doorway, turning to regard the Brother Commander. Sollis was struck by the cautious hesitancy of Arlyn's tone. Although a softly spoken man at most times, his voice rarely lacked certainty.

"Our… former sister," Arlyn said. "She is well?"

"Very well, brother," Elera said.

There was a short interval before Arlyn spoke again. "And the child?"

"As healthy as a new born can be." The sister let out a small laugh. "Perhaps more so."

Another, shorter pause. "Please assure her of my continued friendship and regard when you see her next."

"I shall, brother. Though, I doubt she needs any such reassurance."

The warmth in Elera's voice was coloured by a faint note of something Sollis would never have expected to be directed at Brother Arlyn: pity. Seized by an abrupt sense of transgression, Sollis turned and followed in Artin's wake. He would check on the wounded then spend the hours before sleep pondering a means of surviving his mission. A brief estimation of the odds gave them perhaps one chance in three, though with careful planning and a modicum of luck he thought he might be able to make it an even bet.

CHAPTER THREE

"THE WEED MUST be tested," Sister Elera explained. "I daresay we'll find more than a few plants that bear a similarity to the drawing. I will subject a sample to various agents to ensure it does in fact hold the healing properties we require." She patted the saddle bags on the back of her stout mare before mounting up with a smooth, accustomed grace.

"You could teach me," Sollis said.

"Oh, we certainly don't have time for that." She gave him another of her brisk smiles as she guided her mare towards the first of the inner gates. "You have your task, brother. I have mine."

"This is not a game, sister," he told her.

"Good. I detest games. Such a waste of mental effort." She halted her mare at the gate and glanced over her shoulder, her smile replaced by an impatient frown. "Are you coming?"

Sollis swallowed his anger and turned away. Dealing with someone he couldn't command was always irksome, but Sister Elera was proving a very singular trial. "Brother Lemnish," he said, addressing the youngest of the three brothers waiting with their mounts in the courtyard. "Too many hooves in this party. You'll stay behind."

Sollis saw the young brother mask his relief with a regretful shrug before leading his horse back to the stable. The man was no coward, Sollis knew, but neither was he a fool. "Mount up," he told Oskin and Smentil. Of the two, only Oskin betrayed any outward sign of trepidation and that just a hardly perceptible shake of his head before he climbed into the saddle. They were the two most experienced brothers in the Pass, both having served here for years before Sollis arrived. Risking them on this mission might rob the Order of two of its most valuable assets, but he knew there was little chance of success if he chose to leave them behind.

Vensar, Sollis's own mount, gave only a small snort as he swung himself into the saddle. He had ridden the stallion since being posted to the Pass four years before. The stallion's plains origins were evident in his name, an Eorhil word for a comet that would appear in the northern sky once a century. Sollis assumed it had been chosen for the teardrop blaze of white on the animal's forehead. Despite being bred for the hunt rather than battle, Vensar's mostly sedate nature would disappear in combat, his hooves and teeth proving deadly weapons on more than one occasion.

Red Ears loped ahead as they made their way through the outer walls and the northern gate. The hound never barked, the trait having been bred out of her bloodline generations before. Instead her signals consisted of a sudden stillness, the severity of the threat revealed by the speed at which her tail wagged. Sollis saw her crest a low rise just beyond bowshot of the gate, whereupon she came to an abrupt halt, tail swishing at a slow tempo.

"Well," Oskin said, reining his horse to a halt at the hound's side. "Seems there's something on the wind today."

"The Lonak?" Sister Elera asked.

"No. When she catches their scent her tail becomes straight as an arrow." Oskin angled his head at Red Ears and made a soft clicking sound with his tongue. The hound looked up at him, brows raised, a faint whine escaping her maw. "Something unfamiliar, looks like," Oskin mused, rubbing his grey-stubbled chin. "She doesn't like it, whatever it is."

Sollis spared the hound a brief glance before turning Vensar's nose towards the west. Without any clue as to the nature of whatever alien scent had troubled the hound's nose there seemed little point dwelling on the mystery. "We'll make for the Saw Back," he said. "Cut north once we're through the Notch."

"Forgive me, brother," Elera said as Sollis kicked Vensar into a trot. She prodded her mare to follow suit and quickly drew alongside. "But our destination is to the north-east, is it not? Your course appears to be taking us directly west."

Sollis's eyes flicked to her for an instant before he slapped his reins against Vensar's neck and the stallion accelerated into a gallop. "The mountains have eyes, sister," he heard Oskin explain to Elera. "It doesn't do to follow the compass needle too closely up here."

The Saw Back came into view as the sun neared noon. It was a twenty mile long ridge that rose from the plain to snake a northerly course into the mountains. Centuries before the Renfaelins had named it for its resemblance to the jagged bones of a boar's back, but the Lonak called it Irshak's Tail and believed it to be the remnants of their god of birth. Irshak, so the shamans taught, willingly allowed her spirit to depart her mighty body so that it would sink into the earth, giving rise to the mountains thereby gifting the Lonak a home for all eternity.

Sollis followed the line of the ridge for a mile or so until the Notch came into view. It was a narrow channel that traced a jagged course through the ridge from east to west. Despite being a perfect site for an ambush, the Lonak assiduously avoided the place and no brother had ever been attacked in its vicinity. His attempts to elicit some explanation for this from captives were always met with a scowling refusal to speak a single word on the matter. He wondered if they believed the Notch to be cursed, as if venturing near such a scar in the stone flesh of their dead god was somehow blasphemous. It was likely he would never know and had long resigned himself to the fact that gaining a true understanding of these people was probably impossible.

They dismounted before leading their horses into the Notch. Elera's mare gave voice to some disconcerted snorting as the steep granite walls closed in on either side, but the Order mounts were accustomed to this route and remained quiet. Sollis called a halt about halfway into the Notch where it opened out to create an oval large enough to provide a campsite of sorts.

"Half-moon tonight," Oskin said, gazing up at the mostly grey sky. "Looks like the cloud's inclined to linger for a bit, though."

"Light a fire," Sollis told Smentil before moving to the northern wall of the Notch and starting to climb.

"We're stopping for the night?" Sister Elera asked. "We've barely travelled more than a few miles."

Sollis ignored her and kept climbing.

"And won't a fire reveal our position to the Lonak?" she called after him.

"It's likely they already know our position," he said, not turning. "And will continue to do so as long as you keep shouting."

He ascended to the top of the granite wall and took a moment to scan both the eastern and western approaches, predictably seeing nothing of interest. Sollis faced due north and sat down, closing his eyes and slowing his breathing to allow the song of the mountains to fill his ears. Long years of training at the Order House instilled in him a deep regard for the value of utilising all senses. Today the song was a familiar refrain of swirling winds rebounding from the vast, irregular edifice of the mountains and the rustle and rasp of sparse vegetation. If a Lonak scouting party were to reveal themselves it would be with a small discordant note in the song of the mountains, just a faint series of ticks that indicated unshod hooves on loose stone. Today, however, there were no such ticks. In fact, he found the song unusually muted and it took some time before he detected anything of note.

Hawk, he thought, recognising the faint birdcall, opening his eyes to scan the sky. He found it quickly, a faint speck circling against the grey blanket of cloud. The bird's presence brought a puzzled frown to his brow. Mountain hawks would hunt for mice or rabbits in the foothills, but neither were plentiful at the Saw Back. Also, they would normally only cry out to warn off those who might encroach on their nests, but these were typically found atop the steepest cliffs. It could be trying to attract a mate, though he judged it too late in the season for that.

Sollis watched the hawk until its voice faded and it stopped circling, angling its wings to fly off towards the north. Voicing a soft grunt of frustration at a minor mystery, Sollis rose and climbed back down into the Notch. Brother Smentil had used the firewood from his saddle bags to craft a decent sized blaze, sending a tall column of grey smoke into the dimming sky.

How many? he signed as Sollis moved to unsaddle Vensar.

"None," Sollis replied. He smoothed a hand over the stallion's back before laying the saddle down and extracting a handful of oats from one of the bags. "That I could find, that is."

"Meaning none at all," Oskin said. "Unusual."

"I can't be certain. We need to assume they've spotted us."

"You were expecting the Lonak to find us?" Sister Elera asked which drew an amused glance from Smentil.

We should tie her up and put her on my horse, his hands told Sollis. *He'll make his own way back to the Pass. Any Lonak scouts will most likely leave her be if they still have us to chase after.*

Sister Elera stepped into Smentil's eyeline, face set in a hard mask as her hands moved with swift, if angry fluency. The signs she made were brief though the meaning was colourful and evidently heartfelt.

"I don't think there's any need for that kind of language, sister," Sollis said, holding the oats to Vensar's snout. The stallion let out an appreciative snort as he munched on the snack.

Elera took a slow calming breath, clasping her hands together before speaking again. "Brothers," she began in a tone of measured calm. "I realise I have not your experience in this place, nor do I possess your skills. I am, however, your sister in the Faith and Mistress of Curatives at the House of the Fifth Order. I do not request your respect, I both deserve and expect it. Our mission, as you know, is of the gravest import and I feel its chances of success will be greatly improved if you would be so good as to just answer my bloody questions when I ask them."

Smentil raised an eyebrow in Sollis's direction, receiving a nod in response. Smentil tossed some more sticks onto the fire before turning back to Elera. *If there are any watching,* he signed, *as long as this stays lit they'll believe we're still here.*

"I see," Elera said. "Meaning we'll soon move on and leave it burning."

"We'll wait for darkness," Sollis said. "As long as the moon stays hidden we should be able to head north without being tracked, at least for a while."

"Very clever, brother," she replied, inclining her head a little.

"Cleverness is Brother Sollis's business, sister," Oskin said, sitting down close to the fire and wrapping his cloak about him. "The Grey Eyed Fox the Lonak call him."

"One," Sollis said, seeing his brothers exchange a glance of muted amusement. He was not a man easily baited but had always found the notion of being named by others decidedly annoying, especially his enemies. "One Lonak said that, then he died."

"They tend to do that when you feather them all over with arrows. Mark my words, sister." Oskin cast a wink in Elera's direction. "We travel with a veritable legend. A scourge of Lonak kind."

A stern rebuke came to Sollis's lips but he stilled his tongue. Oskin was a veteran brother who had earned a certain leeway not enjoyed by most of his comrades. Instead, Sollis confined himself to an irritated sigh. "It's a few hours yet until nightfall," he told the sister. "We'll be pushing hard throughout the night. Best unsaddle your horse, we can't afford for her to tire."

NIGHT FELL QUICKLY in the mountains, the sun dipping behind the western peaks to leave the Notch in near-pitch darkness. The clouds had lingered in the sky meaning there was no betraying moonlight as they made their way to the western flank of the Saw Back, the fire burning bright at their rear. The firelight faded as Sollis led them through the cramped passage, guided by touch and memory. The Notch had some side-channels which would trap or delay the unwary but he had memorised the route years before. Soon the granite walls fell away to reveal a broad, rock strewn slope stretching away into the gloom.

Sollis ordered the others to mount up and they struck out for the north, keeping to the upper edge of the slope where it met the crest of the ridge. He spurred Vensar to a steady canter, unwilling to gallop in the darkness. Even so it was a risky endeavour and even a seasoned Order mount like Vensar sometimes came close to losing his footing on the loose stone of the slope. Sister Elera's mare, lacking the same expertise, was less fortunate. Sollis heard the horse let out a shrill whinny and turned to see her sliding down the incline on her rump, forelegs extended as she attempted to stall her descent. Elera held on with valiant resolve, hauling on the reins as shingle cascaded around her.

Horse and rider came to an untidy stop some thirty yards down the slope. Sollis heard the sister give voice to a muffled curse and reined Vensar to a halt, preparing to dismount and go to her aid. He paused, however, at the sound of displaced shingle and fiercely whispered instructions. Peering into the gloom he made out the sight of Elera coaxing her mare into a standing position and slowly guiding her back up the slope. He was impressed with the sister's skill in the saddle, though her stern and embarrassed visage as she fell into line led him to believe any compliments wouldn't be welcome.

"We'll keep to a walk until dawn," he said.

"That's not necessary…" Elera began.

"A walk," Sollis cut in, kicking Vensar forward.

TEN MILES NORTH of the Notch the Saw Back joined the southern flank of a steep-sided mountain, its slopes becoming too sheer for horse or human. Sollis led them around the peak's western base and into a narrow valley marked by the swift stream rushing through its centre. The morning sun soon began to banish the shadows and he spurred Vensar into a gallop, following the line of the stream as it curved towards the east.

He was keen to cover as many miles as possible. They were a decent remove from any sizeable Lonak settlement but he knew it was only a matter of time before a hunting party happened upon their trail. The marks left by steel shod hooves were as good as a signpost in the mountains.

They exited the valley shortly before noon, Sollis slowing the pace as they ascended the forested hills beyond. Once within the trees Oskin sent Red Ears ahead to scout the route, the hound keeping about thirty yards ahead and always staying within sight. After another hour of riding Sollis saw the hound come to a rigid halt, nose pointing off to the right. Her tail wasn't swaying this time, but nor was it straight. Instead, it maintained a steady, nervous twitch.

"She's scenting a beast not a man," Oskin said quietly, brows bunching as he scanned the surrounding trees. "Something with sharp teeth otherwise she wouldn't have stopped."

Sollis nodded to both brothers and all three dismounted, Smentil signing to Elera to follow suit and holding a finger to his lips. The brothers each unlimbered their bows and notched an arrow. Sollis signed for Smentil to stay with the sister and the horses then he and Oskin moved to Red Ears.

"What is it, old pup?" Oskin whispered, crouching at the hound's side and running a hand through the sparse fur on her shoulders.

Red Ears' nose pointed at a dense patch of woodland a dozen paces off, the pines so closely packed as to banish sunlight from the forest floor. A low growl emerged from the hound's muzzle and her lips began to curl, revealing her impressive teeth.

"Rock ape?" Sollis asked Oskin in a low murmur.

The older brother shook his head. "They don't come down from the mountains until winter." The tracker's features took on a familiar frown of concentration, nostrils flaring in unconscious imitation of his dog. "Can't be," he said in a whisper, a bemused squint creeping into his gaze. "Not this far south..."

Sollis saw them then, two small pinpoints of light in the gloom. *Eyes,* he realised. *Cat's eyes catching the light.* His finger tightened on his bowstring as two more pairs of eyes appeared on either side of the first. A grating, piercing squeal cut through the hushed forest air an instant before the cats exploded from the gloom, grey and silver fur flickering as they charged, mouths gaping wide to reveal teeth the length of daggers.

CHAPTER FOUR

S OLLIS ONLY HAD time to half draw his bow, loosing the shaft at a range of less than a yard and sinking the broad steel-head into the cat's mouth. Then it was on him, claws reaching up to clamp onto his shoulders as it sought to stab its elongated teeth into his neck. Sollis rolled with the force of the beast's charge, letting his bow fall from his grip and kicking out with both legs. His boots slammed into the cat's ribcage, propelling it away.

Sollis came to his feet in a crouch, drawing his sword from the scabbard on his back. The cat scrabbled on the ground a few yards away, rasping and shaking its head as it sought to dislodge the arrow jutting from its mouth. Sollis surged forward, bracing the hilt of his sword against his midriff to spear the cat in the chest, blade angled so it made easy passage through the ribcage. It let out a grating, gurgling yowl as the sword point found its heart. Sollis dragged the blade free and stepped away, sparing a moment to watch the cat thrash out its death agonies before whirling to check on his companions.

Another cat was already down, pierced in the chest by two arrows whilst the third was being kept at bay by the combined efforts of Red Ears and Oskin. The pair assailed the beast from two sides, causing it to whirl at each of them in turn, lashing out with its claws as blood leaked from the wounds Oskin's sword left in its flanks. Behind him, Sollis heard the hard thrum of Smentil's bowstring. There was a rush of air and the dark shaft of an arrow appeared in the cat's haunch, causing it to let out a grating, agonised yowl. Its hind quarters became suddenly limp, though it continued to hiss and slash at its assailants until Red Ears darted forward to clamp her jaws on the beast's neck, biting hard. She shook the cat until it sagged into death, limbs twitching.

Sollis retrieved his bow, glancing over to see Smentil notching another arrow. Sister Elera was close behind, clutching the reins of their horses. There was a good deal of fear in her eyes but he detected none of the panicked twitching exhibited by one about to flee.

"Shouldn't be here," Oskin muttered, squinting as he cast his expert eye over each of the fallen cats. Now he had a clear view of them Sollis was impressed by their size, six feet from nose to tail with broad, sharp clawed paws. Then there were the teeth, curved ivory blades eight inches long. He had never seen the like, but Oskin's knowledge of the wilds was far greater than his.

"What are they?" Sollis asked him.

"Snow-daggers," Oskin said. "Least, that's what the Eorhil word for them means in Realm tongue. Never seen one south of the coastal crags."

"And yet here they are," Sollis pointed out.

"Can't rightly explain it, brother." Oskin's normally placid features darkened as he scanned the surrounding trees. "Don't know what's happening here, but it ain't natural." He moved to crouch at the side of the cat Sollis had killed, running a hand over its pelt. "Ribs are near poking through its skin. And the belly's empty. I'd say this beast hasn't had a meal in a good long while."

"Wouldn't that explain why they attacked us?" Elera asked.

"Snow-daggers are solitary beasts, sister," Oskin replied. "Don't hunt in packs, and they're clever enough to avoid the scent of man, no matter how hungry they get." He rose and nodded at Red Ears who was busy worrying at the gash she had torn in the other cat's throat. "Looks like there's no more close by, at least," he said. "She wouldn't be feeding otherwise."

"Even so," Sollis said, turning back to the horses. "I'm unwilling to linger and her meal will have to wait. Mount up. No more stops until nightfall."

THEY COVERED ANOTHER ten miles before the sun began to fade and made camp in the lee of a large, flat topped boulder rising several feet above the treetops. The horses were tethered close by and Sollis took the first watch atop the boulder whilst the others sheltered below. There was no question of lighting a fire this deep into the Lonak dominion and they were obliged to huddle in their cloaks for warmth.

The northerly winds had grown stiff by nightfall, bringing a chill that Sollis's years in the mountains had never quite accustomed him to. Unable to pace for fear of attracting attention, he sat as he maintained his vigil, continually flexing his fingers beneath his cloak. It was never a good idea to draw a sword with a benumbed grip. He counted as he sat, one to three hundred, maintaining a steady cadence. Upon reaching his total he would close his eyes and listen to the song of the mountains for a count of one hundred. It was a trick the Master of the Wild had taught him during his time at the Order House, a means of occupying the mind without losing concentration, and it had saved his life more than once.

It was during his fifth repetition that he heard it again: the hawk's call, more distant this time but unmistakably the same, plaintive cry. His eyes snapped open, ranging across the sky in search of the bird. The cloud cover was thinner now and the half-moon bright against the black of the sky. *What manner of hawk flies at night?* he wondered, finding no trace of a winged shape anywhere. The question brought Oskin's words to mind: *ain't natural.* Sollis began to rise, intending to wake Oskin for an opinion, then paused as a faint scent reached his nostrils. *Smoke,* he thought, lowering his gaze to the surrounding landscape. He found the source quickly, a blaze atop a low hill perhaps five miles north.

Hearing a scrape of leather on stone he turned to find Sister Elera clambering up onto the boulder, gazing at the distant fire with a wary expression. "A signal fire?" she asked.

"No," Sollis said. "The Lonak don't use them. You should be resting."

She gave a sheepish shrug. "I couldn't sleep. And I smelt the smoke." She nodded at the yellow-orange smudge in the distance. "If it's not a signal, what is it?"

Sollis returned his attention to the blaze. It was large, sending a tall column of thick smoke into the night sky. It was also a good deal above the trees which meant at least it wouldn't spread. "There's a village on that hilltop," he said. "It appears to be burning."

"A battle?" she wondered. "The clans war amongst themselves, Brother Arlyn said."

"It's possible," Sollis conceded. "But I've never seen them burn a whole village before. It's not their warriors' habit to kill the young or the old, unless they're Merim Her, of course."

"Merim Her?"

"It's what they call us. It roughly translates as 'sea-scum'."

"I see. A reference to our forebear's seaborne migration all those centuries ago, I presume. It's said the Lonak and the Seordah once had dominion over all the lands that now comprise the Realm."

"Then we came and took it all away. It's hardly surprising they're still somewhat bitter."

Sollis lifted his gaze to the sky once more, resuming his search for the hawk but finding nothing. The bird's unnatural nighttime flight in close proximity to the burning village was enough of a troubling coincidence to dictate their next course, albeit one he would have preferred to avoid.

"In the morning," he said, "we will inspect what remains of that village."

"Wouldn't it be better to go around?" Elera said. "Whoever attacked it may still be in the vicinity, may they not?"

"Two bucks with one arrow," he reminded her. "You have your mission and I have mine. Please sister, get some sleep."

THEY FOUND THE first body halfway up the sloping track that led to the village. A girl, perhaps thirteen years old, lying face down with an arrow in her back. *She was running,* Smentil signed as he examined the corpse with a critical eye. *From the depth of the shaft I'd put the range at over a hundred paces. In the dark too. Quite a feat.* He crouched and reached out to run his fingers over the fletching.

"Gull feathers," Oskin observed. "Looks a good deal like one of ours."

The quill isn't flush with the shaft, Smentil signed, shaking his head. *No brother's hand made this.*

"But I'd hazard whoever did wanted the Lonak to think otherwise," Sollis concluded. He looked towards the top of the slope where a dim pall of smoke mingled with the dense morning mist. The points of the sharpened logs forming the village stockade were just visible above the crest, a long row of blackened teeth in the murk.

"Anything?" he asked Oskin, nodding at Red Ears. The hound's tail swished continually, though the direction of her nose wavered.

"Just death, I think," Oskin said. "And no small amount of it either."

Sollis and his brothers notched arrows before approaching the entrance to the village at a slow walk whilst Elera followed closely behind, leading the horses. The familiar stench of the recently dead mingled with charred wood as Sollis paused amidst the ruins of what had been the gate. The large oakwood doors that had guarded this settlement were now shattered and blackened splinters. Beyond them much of the rest of the village was shrouded in mist, but he could see the bodies of a dozen Lonak lying nearby, men and women. A variety of spears, knives and war clubs lay amongst them and their wounds told of an intense close-quarters fight. Most were only partially dressed and Sollis deduced they had been roused from sleep by the attack.

Came running to defend the gate, Smentil signed. *I'd guess it had already fallen when they got here.*

"Brother," Oskin said, nodding to another corpse just beyond the gate, a corpse clad in a blue cloak. Sollis moved quickly to examine the body, finding an unfamiliar, pale complexioned face beneath a shock of close-cropped black hair. The man had a sword of the Asraelin pattern lying close to his hand and a hatchet buried in the thin leather armour that covered his chest.

"Done up like a brother, sure enough," Oskin observed. "Not well enough to convince anyone with an experienced eye, though."

Sollis scrutinised the rest of the dead man's clothing, finding the boots and leather armour of unfamiliar design. A cursory glance at the man's hands confirmed them as rough and strong, the hands of a warrior, but of what stripe?

He looked up as Smentil tapped him on the shoulder and motioned for him to move aside. When Sollis had done so the brother knelt to draw the hatchet from the dead man's chest then unfastened his armour, pulling it aside. Using his hunting knife he sliced through the wool shirt beneath to reveal a pattern of old scars scored into the man's flesh.

Volarian, his hands said. *Slave-soldier.*

"Seen this before, brother?" Oskin asked him.

Years ago, Smentil replied. *After a fight with some Meldenean pirates. They had taken a Volarian ship and were sailing it to the Isles. Hadn't got round to throwing the bodies overboard when we hove into view.*

"Then this fellow's come a very long way." Oskin retreated a few steps, shrewd eyes scanning the village. "Another one over there." He pointed to a second blue-cloaked figure lying some twenty yards on. A closer inspection revealed the same complexion and scar pattern beneath his armour. However, the cause of his death was different, a large gaping hole in his throat Oskin judged to be the result of a bite.

"Another snow-dagger?" Sollis suggested but Oskin shook his head.

"They puncture the throat and suffocate their prey." He moved away, eyes narrowed in concentration as he surveyed the muddy ground. "This was something with different teeth, and bigger." He paused and sank to his haunches, fingers reaching out to hover over a mark. "Much bigger…" he murmured, Sollis detecting a faint note of incredulity in his tone.

"It looks like a wolf print," he said, looking over Oskin's shoulder, although the size of the track made him wonder. It was at least twice the breadth and width of any wolf's paw he had ever seen.

"That it is," Oskin agreed, rising and moving forward, eyes fixed on the ground. "Got quite the stride, this fellow." He came to a halt several yards on, nodding at an overlapping matrix of tracks. "Looks like he paused here, then…" Oskin turned, striding towards the stockade. Sollis followed him through the gap between two huts whereupon they both drew up short at the sight before them. A large ragged hole had been torn in the timbers of the stockade. It was both wide and tall enough to allow the passage of a full grown man, or something of equal size.

"Faith," Oskin whispered, staring at the jagged edges of the hole. "What could do this?"

"The splinters are all on the inside of the wall," Sollis noted.

Oskin's gaze immediately returned to the ground. "It came in this way." His finger traced a route from the stockade to the village, then back again. "Killed one of the slave-soldiers, paused for a second or two then left the same way." He shook his head in grim-faced bafflement. "Why, brother? What unearthly thing has happened here?"

"Not so much an unearthly thing, brother." Sollis peered through the hole at the misted landscape beyond. "A Dark thing."

Oskin gave a perturbed grunt and moved to survey the ground beyond the hole. "Bare rock all around. Little chance of tracking it, whatever it…"

He fell silent at the sound of shouting to their rear. Sollis and Oskin raised their bows and swiftly retraced their steps. Sister Elera came into view first, standing with her arms outstretched in the wide thoroughfare that ran through the centre of the village. Smentil stood to her right, his bow drawn and arrow aimed at something to her left, though she moved continually in an obvious attempt to frustrate his aim.

"Put that down!" she commanded, though Smentil seemed disinclined to obey.

Sollis rounded one of the huts, preparing to draw his own bow then pausing at the sight of the three figures behind Elera. An old, stick thin Lonak man stood shielding two small children, a boy and a girl. All three were glaring at Elera and Smentil with a mix of fear and defiant hatred. Upon catching sight of Sollis the old man began to mutter a death song, pulling the two children closer to his side as he did so.

"Brother," Sollis said, lowering his bow and shaking his head at Smentil. The brother slowly relaxed his bowstring as Sollis stepped past him. The trio of Lonak tensed as he approached, the children's faces bunching, though the old man held them in place and they made no attempt to flee. He straightened his back as Sollis came to a halt a few yards away, snarling a rebuke at the little boy when he let out a sob.

"*Isk-reh varn kha-il dohim ser varkhim ke!*" *Do not blight our death with your weakness!*

Sollis saw that the old man held something, a crumpled, ragged edged length of tanned goatskin, clutched tight in his bony fist. Drawing closer Sollis recognised the markings stitched into the skin: *war banner*. Slowly, he removed the arrow from his bow and returned it to his quiver, holding the weapon up and raising his other hand, fingers spread wide. "We do not bring death this day," he said in Lonak.

"Why not?" the old man enquired, lips curled. "When you brought so much last night?"

Sollis looked around at the ruined village with its blackened, roofless huts and many corpses. "We didn't do this," he said.

"Lies!" the old man spat. He raised a fist to brandish the war banner at Sollis. "Kill us and have done, but do not soil my ears with Merim Her tricks."

"These men," Sollis went on, pointing to the blue-cloaked corpse lying nearby, "they wear our garb, but they are not from our lands. We have come to end them."

Sollis saw the old man's eyes twitch then, betraying a certain sly glint as he straightened a little, saying, "Then you are too late. The Varnish Dervakhim have already ended them all."

Sollis's gaze snapped to Red Ears as she let out a soft whine. The hound's nose was pointed towards the ruined gate, tail straight and unwavering. A half-dozen figures stood amidst the ruins of the gate, features obscured by the mist but evidently Lonak judging by their weapons and garb. A slender figure stood at their head. This one carried no weapons, regarding Sollis with head titled and arms folded in apparently careful scrutiny.

"Brother," Oskin said softly, Sollis hearing his bow creak as he drew the string taut. Turning in a slow circle Sollis saw other Lonak emerging from the ruins, some with lowered spears, others drawn flat-bows. He quickly counted at least twenty with more appearing behind. *Too many,* he knew, grinding his teeth in self-reproach.

"Sister," he said to Elera. "You were right. We should have gone around."

"Thank you, brother," she replied in an admirably steady tone.

"When it starts," he went on, reaching for his quiver as the

Lonak inched closer, "mount up and ride off, as fast as you can. We should be able to create enough of a distraction for you to get clear. If it appears they're about to catch you, I advise that you cut your wrists. A downward stroke works best."

"Your concern is appreciated, brother."

His fingers closed on an arrow and his gaze fixed on the closest Lonak, a stocky warrior now only twenty yards away. The man's features were set in the hard mask of imminent combat, his own bow fully drawn. There were two more behind, one with a club, the other a spear. Sollis was confident he could get two with his arrows before dispatching the third with his sword. After that…

"*Reh–isk!*" *Stop!*

Sollis's gaze swung towards the gate where the slender figure was now striding forward, arms unfolded and waving dismissively at the encroaching Lonak. At the command they came to a sudden halt, although their bows remained drawn and spears lowered. As the figure came closer Sollis saw that it was a woman. A pelt of wild-cat fur covered her torso, though her lean, muscled arms were bare, each richly decorated in tattoos. A long scalp-lock traced from the top of her head and down her back. Sollis was quick to recognise the green and red ink pattern covering most of her shaven head: *shaman.*

She came to a halt a dozen feet away, looking at each of them in turn. Sollis was struck by the lack of animosity on her face, she was even smiling a little. "Hello," she said in perfect Realm tongue, the accent every bit as smooth and cultured as Sister Elera's. Her eyes tracked over each of them again before coming to rest on Sollis, whereupon she frowned, lips pursed in apparent disappointment. "She said you would be taller."

FIVE

"T HEY'RE CALLED KURITAI," the shaman said, kicking
the blue-cloaked corpse at her feet. "The Volarian slave-
elite. Deadly but mindless."

The other Lonak had retreated after she barked out a series
of harsh commands. They still maintained a perimeter around
Sollis and the others, but had at least relaxed their bows and
lowered their spears. From the hard, hate-filled glares on every
face Sollis deduced that the only thing keeping them from a
swift and merciless slaughter was the authority enjoyed by this
strange woman.

"And what do they call you?" he asked her.

"Verkehla," she replied, turning to him with a smile and bowing. "Tahlessa to the Varnish Dervakhim, by the word of the Mahlessa."

Verkehla, Sollis searched his memory for the meaning. *Bloody Arrow.* "I am…" he began but she cut him off.

"Brother Sollis of the Sixth Order," she said, eyebrows raised in a mockery of awe. "The Grey Eyed Fox himself. I am truly honoured."

Sollis heard Oskin let out a soft laugh before muttering, "Told you, brother."

"Varnish Dervakhim," Sollis went on, ignoring him. "The Outcast Knives?"

"Your translation is somewhat inelegant," Verkehla replied. "I prefer 'The Banished Blades.' A tad more poetic, don't you think?"

He gestured to the surrounding Lonak. "These are all Varnish?"

"Indeed they are." Verkehla's face took on a sour expression as she surveyed her fellow Lonak. "Murderers, thieves, liars and oath-breakers. All given a chance at redemption by the Mahlessa's word. They make for fairly terrible company, I must say. I find I hate them all quite a lot." Her features bunched into a sudden, resentful snarl and she called out in Lonak, "I just told him how much I hate you, you worthless ape-fuckers!"

This caused many of the onlooking Lonak to stiffen and focus their baleful glares on the shaman instead of the four Merim Her. However, Sollis noted that although their hands tightened on their weapons, not one voice was raised against her. Every warrior suffered the insult in rigid silence.

"See?" Verkehla said. "They'd dearly love to kill me, almost as much as they'd delight in killing you. But they'll put up with pretty much anything, just for the merest chance the Mahlessa might restore them to their clans."

"I assume this is the reason why we aren't currently fighting," Sollis said, nodding again at the corpse she had named a Kuritai.

Verkehla met his gaze, smiling and saying nothing for a moment that stretched as her eyes shifted from him to Sister Elera. "You're a healer, aren't you?" she asked.

"I am," the sister replied. "Sister Elera of the Fifth Order..."

"Yes, all very nice and fine, I'm sure," Verkehla broke in. "We have wounded. Will you attend to them?"

"Of course."

The shaman turned and barked out more commands at the surrounding Lonak. "Find a dwelling that still has a roof, and gather the wounded there. The Merim Her bitch will see to them, and I don't want to hear any grumbling about it."

She fixed her gaze on Sollis once again. "Whilst your sister does her compassionate duty, you and I will share stories at the fire. I'm sure you have an interesting tale to tell."

"SNOW-DAGGERS, EH?" Verkehla raised an eyebrow in surprise as she chewed on a roasted rabbit. They sat together in a ruined hut, alone apart from the old man and the two children. Sollis had ordered Smentil and Oskin to stay at Elera's side, although Verkehla assured him they were in no danger. A fire blazed in the central pit that served as a focal point for all Lonak dwellings, a brace of freshly slaughtered rabbits roasting on a spit above the flames. The roof had been claimed by the blaze the night before and smoke rose through the blackened rafters into a grey sky. The children huddled at the old man's side as they sat in a corner, chewing on the meat Verkehla had tossed to them and staring at Sollis with bright, fearful eyes.

"We call them *kavim kiral*," she went on. "Shadow-cats, because they're so rarely seen, especially this far south. One of many strange occurrences recently."

"We found no sign of any other Lonak," Sollis said. "Until now. Also very strange in my experience."

Verkehla gave a small grin. "They're all at home, on the Mahlessa's order. Word came from the Mountain that no war bands or hunting parties were to venture out for a full month."

"Apart from your Banished Blades."

"Quite. They are…" She paused, frowning. "Expendable, I believe the term is."

"It is. You know our language very well."

"I had a fine education." The grin disappeared from her lips and Sollis noted a hard cast creep into her eyes. Clearly, this was an unwelcome topic of conversation.

"You said something about me being taller," Sollis said. "You were expecting us."

"Just you, actually. The other three are a complication, especially your blonde sister. I can't imagine what possessed you to bring her into the mountains."

"We have a mission. And she's hardier than she looks."

"She'll need to be." Verkehla bit the last morsel of meat from the rabbit's haunch and tossed the bone into the fire, wiping the grease from her face with the back of her hand. "The Mahlessa, in her wisdom, has foreseen your coming, oh fox of the grey eyes. As she foresaw the coming of those who would wear your garb and do murder in your name. Quite where and when was not revealed to her, and so I and my company of scum were despatched to hunt them down."

"So your mission is complete?"

"Hardly." Verkehla let out a sigh and glanced at the children, causing them to huddle closer to the old man. "Not while these two are still drawing breath, at least."

"They are important?" Sollis asked.

"Apparently. Or at least one of them is. The Mahlessa's statements regarding the visions she receives from the Gods can be… vague. Like a riddle that needs a good deal of pondering before it's solved. 'They come for the child,' she said, sadly without providing a name for said child. All she could tell me is that they live in this village, and that someone has brought the Dark into these mountains to kill them."

"Perhaps this child has already perished," Sollis suggested. "There are corpses of all ages littering this place."

Verkehla shook her head, gaze lingering on the children. "No. Whatever it is waits nearby, watches. I can feel it. We killed its slave-soldiers, but it's not done. It'll come for them. Be sure of that, brother."

"How?" He squinted at her in bafflement as her gaze swung back to him. "How can you *feel* it?"

She blinked and shifted her eyes to the fire, remaining silent for long enough to allow Sollis to conclude this was another question she wouldn't answer. Finally, she said, "You mentioned a mission. Might I enquire what it is? Since you brought a healer I don't imagine you've ventured forth with assassination in mind."

Sollis pondered the wisdom of sharing his knowledge with her, deciding it couldn't do any harm. "There's a place," he said. "We call it Morvil's Reach. We need to find something there, a plant with healing properties."

Verkehla let out a soft snort of amusement. "You came into our lands to look for a plant? The Mahlessa's riddle told of a quest of fabled proportions. I was at least hoping for buried treasure. Or perhaps a lost, Dark-imbued sword from the time of the ancients."

"Sorry to disappoint you."

She shrugged and got to her feet. "No matter. We'll go with you to the Reach. We call it *Trehl kha lahk dehvar*, incidentally."

"The hilltop of the... wrong headed man?" Sollis asked, struggling with the translation.

"The Mad Man's Stockade," she corrected, shaking her head. "You certainly have a gift for mangling our language, brother." She turned to address the old man in Lonak. "Can you still fight, or is it time to leave you out in the snow?"

"I can fight," he replied, chin jutting in pique. He raised the ragged goatskin in his hand, unfurling it to reveal the markings. "Do you not know who you behold, oh Servant of the Mountain? Do you not know this banner? I am Khela-hahk, the bloody club, the Shatterer of Skulls, last of the Stone Crushers. We who stood alone against the steel-clads at the Black River. We who laid low a *kermana* of Merim Her in a single day..."

"Never heard of you," Verkehla broke in. "And since you're still alive, I'd guess you didn't do much skull shattering last night. Find a midden to hide in, did you?"

The old man glared at her, bony jaw bunching in suppressed fury as he lowered the banner to draw the two children closer still. "They required my protection," he said.

"Are they your blood?" she asked, angling her head to survey the infants.

"I was blood-father to their mother." His fury abated a little as he lowered his gaze. "She died fighting those who wore this one's garb." He jerked his head at Sollis. "And you act as if he is not our enemy. You share stories at the fire with a Blue-cloak. What a vile, shameful thing…"

"Word from the Mountain is not to be questioned," Verkehla snapped, causing the old man to fall into an abrupt silence. "Besides," she added, turning back to Sollis with a skeptical half-grin, "according to the Mahlessa he's going to be your whelps' valiant protector."

THEY DEPARTED THE village at noon, Verkehla and the Banished Blades mounting up on sturdy ponies and trotting through the ruined gate. The corpses of their fellow Lonak were left where they lay, as was the custom in the mountains. "They belong to the Gods now," Verkehla said when Sister Elera enquired about Lonak funeral customs. "They will ordain how their flesh is disposed of." Sollis noticed that the woman's arch, often cynical inflection disappeared when she spoke of the gods. Apparently, the subject of the divine was one thing she took very seriously.

"I don't think he relishes our company," Elera observed, nodding at the old man's continually scowling visage. He and his two grandchildren were mounted on spare ponies and trotted at the rear of the company alongside Sollis and his fellow Merim Her.

"Too right he doesn't, sister," Oskin agreed with a chuckle. "Nothing would make him happier than slitting our throats." He raised his voice, leaning towards the old man as he asked, "Isn't that right, you old savage?"

The old man's lips curled in anger and he spat back with a few choice insults of his own. Much of it was too fast for Sollis to catch, although he did detect the words 'horse-fucking cock-swallower'.

"Leave him be, brother," Sollis instructed. "And his name's Khela-hahk."

Oskin swung to him with a quizzical frown then shrugged as he saw Sollis's intent sincerity. "Couldn't give a rat's balls for his name, brother," Oskin muttered, spurring his horse forward. "But as you wish."

"Servants of the Faith should be beyond hatred," Elera commented to Sollis, a judgmental cast to her eyes as she regarded Oskin.

"It's easier to keep to the catechisms when you spend your life in warm rooms under a sound roof, sister," Sollis replied. "And when you haven't had to carry a dozen murdered children to the fire and speak the words for them, because their parents have also been murdered."

Her gaze swung to him, narrowing yet further. "So you hate them too?"

Sollis frowned, finding it odd that the notion of how he felt about the Lonak had never occurred to him before. "No more than I hate these mountains from which I might fall one day, or the wind that could steal the warmth of my body on a stormy night. The Lonak are simply the most dangerous threat in a place full of dangers. But," he paused to incline his head at a still glowering Khela-hahk, "regardless of how we might feel about them, they will always hate us. Even the shaman who leads this band. She might speak our language and understand our customs better than any of her kind, but she hates us too. I see it clearly."

"Then why are they helping us?"

"Perhaps they aren't." Sollis looked at the two children perched back to back on a pony. The boy, marginally the older of the two, returned Sollis's gaze with a fierce, suspicious glower, whilst the girl simply stared back in puzzled curiosity. "Perhaps," Sollis added softly, "we're helping them. But to what end I cannot say."

SIX

THE MAD MAN'S Stockade," Verkehla said. She reined her pony to a halt, pointing to a steep hill rising from the floor of a shallow valley a mile or so ahead. The stronghold of Morvil's Reach lay atop the hill, its dark, weather beaten walls more intact than Sollis had expected. Noting that the western and northern approaches were guarded by the hooked bend of a fast flowing river, Sollis concluded that whatever the failings of the unfortunate Lord Morvil, he had at least possessed an eye for a sound defensive position.

"Your people left the stones in place," he observed to Verkehla who shrugged.

"The Grey Hawks shun the place," she said. "There are old stories about the spectres of Merim Her wandering the place on dark nights, crying out to be let into the Beyond. It seems the Departed have barred entry, possibly due to the shame of their defeat."

"You know the Faith?" Elera asked her. Her tone was one of gratified surprise but Verkehla turned to her with a harsh glare.

"Far better than I would like, sister," she said, baring her teeth in a harsh mutter. Elera blanched a little but didn't look away, straightening the saddle and forming her features into a neutral mask.

"The Departed are rarely so judgmental," Sollis said, nudging Vensar forward to place him between the shaman and the healer. "Those who die in honest battle can expect a place in the Beyond."

"Honest battle?" Verkehla's expression softened into one of amused scorn as she shifted her gaze to Sollis. "There was a small settlement on this hill before your people came. What do you imagine their fate to have been? Perhaps your Departed simply refused entry to a gang of murderers and thieves."

"Getting dark," Oskin said, voice gruff with impatience. "Be best if we got ourselves within those walls and settled for the night, look for the sister's precious weed in the morning."

Sollis raised a questioning eyebrow at Verkehla who nodded and spurred her pony forward, barking a command at the Varnish Dervakhim. "Spread out and scout all approaches. I want to know about any track you find, however small."

As the Lonak fanned out she led Sollis and the others along a mostly overgrown trail that led to the stronghold's gate.

He judged the height of the walls at a little over twenty feet, overlooked by a single tower. The iron braced oak doors lay in rusted ruin, revealing a small courtyard of moss-covered rock beyond. The tower rose from the centre of the courtyard, its unusually wide base indicating it had served a dual role as main keep and lookout post.

Typical Renfaelin design, Smentil signed as he surveyed the structure. *Just a good deal smaller than usual.*

"Shall we, brother?" Verkehla asked Sollis, dismounting and gesturing at the unbarred gate. She started inside without waiting for an answer. Sollis told the others to stay put and climbed down from Vensar's back, handing the reins to Smentil before following the shaman inside.

"I can't see any spectres," she commented, standing in the centre of the courtyard and scanning the narrow battlements above. "Perhaps it's a tad too early for them, eh?"

Sollis ignored the jibe, one hand on the hilt of his sword as he moved in a slow circle, eyes probing every shadowed corner of the stronghold's interior. "You walk into potential danger with no weapon," he said. "That is unwise. There could be more slave-soldiers waiting in ambush."

"There aren't," she replied with casual certainty. "We killed them all. And trust me, brother, when I say I am far from defenceless."

Despite her words Sollis insisted on a thorough inspection of the structure before allowing the others inside. He found himself impressed with the solidity of the place, the precision with which the stones had been laid and aligned told of skilled hands.

"Lord Morvil knew his business in one respect at least," he commented to his brothers later. They sat together in the base of the tower around a small fire that sent a column of smoke into the skeletal rafters above. He had pondered the wisdom of lighting a fire that would be sure to advertise their presence here. However, the Dervakhim seemed oblivious to such concerns, those not posted to the walls clustering around their own fires as they roasted meat and followed their nightly ritual of sharing stories.

"Or, more likely his masons did," Oskin replied. "Poor bastards, following their lord to this forsaken place. It's safe odds they died along with all his knights and retainers. I hope he paid them well in the meantime."

Sollis's attention was drawn to the opposite side of the fire by an unusual sound, one he realised he hadn't heard in these mountains before. The little Lonak girl was laughing, small hands over her mouth as she regarded Elera with wide, delighted eyes. "Sermahkash," the sister said, smiling in bemusement as this provoked another round of giggling from the girl. "It's her name," she said, catching sight of Sollis's quizzical frown. "At least I think so."

"Your pronunciation is a little off, sister," Sollis said. "Sumehrkas. It means Misted Dawn. The way you said it resembled the Lonak word for ape piss."

"Oh." Elera laughed and poked the girl gently in the belly. "Are you making fun of me, little one?"

The girl laughed again then fell abruptly silent as Khela-hahk uttered a curt rebuke. He and the boy sat together at another fire a few feet away, the old man beckoning to the girl with a stern frown on his wrinkled brow. She gave a sullen pout and rose from Elera's side, starting forward then halting as the sister gently took her hand. "We're only playing…" she began, offering the old warrior a reassuring smile.

"Sister," Sollis said softly, shaking his head. Elera sighed and released the girl who stomped to the other fire, slumping down with arms crossed and face set in sulky reproach.

"Don't feel too bad, sister," Oskin commented, chewing a mouthful of dried beef. "Probably just trying to win your trust so she can slit your throat when you're sleeping."

"What a fount of unsolicited opinions you are, brother," Elera observed with a thin smile.

"We know what these people are," Oskin returned evenly. "You do not and would do well to listen to experienced counsel." He jerked his head at Smentil who sat running a whetstone over the blade of his sword. "Ask our brother. They held him for ten days, visited all manner of outrages on his flesh, not to say taking his tongue into the bargain. It astonishes me he can stomach being in their company."

Smentil's whetstone emitted a harsh grind as he scraped it the length of the blade, his eyes fixing Oskin with a glare of warning. The older brother flushed a little and lowered his gaze. "Apologies, brother," he murmured.

"As ever, idle hands make for useless talk," Sollis said, adopting a brisk tone as he rose, hefting his bow and settling his sword on his back. "Brother Oskin, take your hound and scout beyond the walls. The Lonak didn't find any suspicious tracks but that doesn't mean much this deep in the mountains. Stay within bowshot of the walls. Brother Smentil will go with you. Sister." He inclined his head at Elera. "My earlier inspection revealed something I believe may be of interest to our mission, if you would care to join me."

DESPITE BEING CRACKED in places, the winding stairs that hugged the wall of the building were another testament to the soundness of the fortress's construction, remaining intact all the way to the top. Sollis guided their steps with a flaming torch as Elera followed him into the tower's gloomy upper reaches.

"For all his prejudice," she said, "Brother Oskin makes an insightful point. Smentil seems remarkably free of hatred towards our new companions."

"He was always a difficult man to read," Sollis replied. "Even in the days when he could speak. In any case, the Faith teaches us that vengeance is folly, does it not?"

"'A vindictive heart stains the Beyond,'" she agreed with a quote. "As set down in The Catechism of Truth. Perhaps Oskin should pay greater attention to its message."

Sollis resisted the impulse to impart a brief summation of the many trials Oskin had suffered since his deployment to the Pass, knowing it to be an excuse. *What is the point of Faith if it is to be abandoned in the face of adversity?* he pondered, silently resolving to speak to Brother Commander Arlyn when they returned. Perhaps it was time for Oskin to take up a master's role at the Order House where he could impart his wisdom to the next generation of novice brothers.

"In here," he said, pausing at a narrow doorway. He lowered the torch to illuminate the interior, gesturing for her to precede him.

"Hardly a grand chamber," Elera said, casting her gaze around the room which was ten feet across at its widest point. "You truly think this was where Lord Morvil held court?"

"No, but I'd hazard this is where he slept. Small as it is, it's still the largest chamber in the whole fortress." Sollis followed her inside, glancing back at the doorway before lowering his voice. "I noticed something," he said, moving to the far wall and crouching. "Something I thought it best the Lonak woman didn't see."

He pointed to a mark on the brickwork an inch from the floor. It was small but neatly chiselled into the stone, a rectangular symbol inset with two dots. "Is that..?" Elera began, leaning down and squinting at the marking.

"Far Western script," Sollis said. "I believe it means 'book'."

"You can read Far Western script, brother?"

Sollis chose not to take offence at the keen surprise in her voice. Why would a brother of the Sixth know such things, after all? "Not in its entirety, no," he admitted. "But I've had occasion to fight smugglers and pirates, some of Far Western origin. They tend to mark their hiding places with symbols such as these, believing, not without good reason, that easterners are too ignorant to recognise them as anything but a meaningless scrawl."

"So, you think Lord Morvil learned the same trick?"

"The accounts of his life are colourful, full of unlikely tales of adventures in far-off lands. Perhaps some of it was actually true."

Elera let out a small laugh, shuffling closer to run her fingers over the symbol. Sollis made a conscious effort not to notice the soft caress of her hair on his neck as she did so. "It occurs to me your knowledge and intellect might have been better employed in the Third Order," she murmured.

"I doubt it." Sollis drew the hunting knife from his belt and worked the tip of the blade into the mortar that bound the marked brick in place. "This might take some time," he said, handing her the torch. "If you would care to guard the door."

"Of course."

It took close on an hour's labour to loosen the brick, Sollis doggedly scraping away the mortar until he had sufficient room to work his fingers into the gap and lever the stone free. "The torch, sister," he said, extending his hand as he lowered himself to peer into the small space. He gave a small grunt of satisfaction as the torchlight revealed the dim gleam of a leather binding. Reaching in, he extracted a small volume, the cover and spine lacking any inscription. The leather that bound it was dry and cracked with age, flaking into powder as Sollis ran his fingers over it.

"I think this calls for gentler hands," he said, handing the book to Elera.

The sister carefully opened the book, revealing pages of yellow parchment inscribed in a flowing, elegant script. Despite the precision of the penmanship Sollis found he couldn't read a word of it. "That's not Realm Tongue," he said.

"'The Conquest of the Northern Mountains and the Subjugation of the Wolf Men'," Elera read, her finger tracing across the words inscribed at the top of the first page. "'Being a true and honest account by Baron Valeric Morvil, Knight of Renfael.'" She raised a caustic eyebrow. "Clearly a fellow not lacking in self-regard." She smiled at Sollis's puzzled frown. "It's ancient Volarian, brother. At one time all scholarly works in the four fiefs were written in this script. In fact, it remained a common practice amongst the more pretentious scholars until King Janus banned its use during the first year of his reign."

"And yet, you can read it," Sollis observed.

"My..." she began then paused, Sollis recognising the familiar expression of a servant of the Faith reminding themselves that mention of one's previous life was frowned upon. "I learned a great deal before I entered the Order," she added, returning her attention to the book. "The first few pages relate his preparations for the campaign, buying of provisions, hiring of men and so on." She thumbed ahead, grimacing in consternation. "It seems the Baron's self-regard is matched only by his verbosity. It will take several hours to fully examine this for mention of the weed."

"Very well." Sollis moved to the door. "Best find a quiet corner to do so. I'd prefer the Lonak not see you with it."

"They object to books?"

"No, they love them, or rather their Mahlessa does. When they raid the only booty they prize more than horses are books. Apparently, the Mountain provides great rewards for any warrior who comes to offer books in tribute. If they see you with that, they'll almost certainly try to take it."

Elera nodded and consigned the book to the inner folds of her robe. "Do you believe her?" she asked. "That whatever or whoever destroyed that village is still out there."

"I do. In fact, I suspect it's why we're still alive. The Mahlessa has ordered it, at least as long as the threat to her people persists."

"A threat she saw in some Dark vision?" Elera shook

her head. "I find it hard to credit mere superstition for our predicament, brother."

"What is superstition to us is real to them. The Mahlessa believes, and therefore so do they, that we have a role to play in ending the evil infesting these mountains. Even should we find the weed, I doubt we'll be going anywhere until this vision has come to pass. We are expected to spring a trap, and those children downstairs are but bait."

"And therefore deserving of our protection, wouldn't you say?"

Sollis saw a glint of wary appraisal in her gaze then, as if her question were a test and she feared he might fail it. "Rest assured, sister," he said. "I'll defend them as I would any child, Realm born, Faithful or not."

She gave a tight smile, stepping forward to place a hand on his, her flesh warm despite the chill that pervaded the fortress. "I must confess to always having harboured a certain... discomfort with the need for your Order," she said. "Why should a Faith that celebrates life require servants so skilled in the ways of death? I see now, my questions were misplaced..."

She fell silent as he raised a hand, his gaze drawn upwards by a new sound, a faint and plaintive call drifting through the part destroyed roof of the tower. "What is that?" Elera asked.

"Hawk," Sollis said, handing her the torch. "Make your way back down, sister. I'll be there shortly."

The faint moonlight enabled him to navigate to the tower's roof without undue difficulty where he found Verkehla waiting, head tilted at an expectant angle. "You and the sister spent a good deal of time alone, brother," she observed. "What could you have been doing?"

"Discussing the finer points of the Catechism of Truth," Sollis replied, ascending the last few steps onto the patchy stonework that formed the tower's summit. The thick beams that supported the wall could be seen through gaps in the floor, like the exposed ribs of a massive rotting corpse. The top was ringed by a low crenellated wall which remained weathered but intact. Sollis moved to it, eyes raised to the partly clouded sky and ears alive for the hawk's call.

"So you heard it too?" Verkehla asked. "A cry in the night from a bird that never flies in darkness."

"Not just tonight," he said. "I've heard it three times now, once not long before we were attacked by the snow-daggers."

"Information you might have shared with me earlier."

Sollis glanced at her judgmental frown and gave a faint shrug. "And have you shared all your pertinent information with me?"

Her face took on an impassive aspect that told of another refusal to answer so he returned his gaze to the sky. "No sign of it," he murmured.

"It's there. Whatever commands it will make sure it keeps watch on us."

"Commands it?"

Evidently his skepticism showed in his voice for her tone was curt when she replied, "You are quite willing to believe the ghosts of the dead gather together in some mystical, invisible realm, and yet you shun evidence of what you call the Dark when it stares you in the face."

"Your people shun it, do they not?"

"Yes, because they have the wit to recognise the danger it poses. Your people hide behind scorn or choose to blame the Dark on those who deny the Faith, a Faith that preaches peace yet is quite happy to cage heretics and hang them from a gibbet to starve. Ever had to do that, brother?"

Sollis had as yet been spared the duty of accompanying the Third Order on their Denier hunting expeditions. Even so, there were many stories from brothers who had, and they were far from edifying. "No," he said.

"But you would," she persisted. "If your Order commanded it, you would."

"The Faith requires all we have. As your Mahlessa, I'm sure, requires all of you."

She began to answer but halted as a harsh scream cut through the night air beyond the battlement, quickly followed by the shouts and snapping bowstrings that told of combat. Sollis immediately unslung his bow, notching an arrow as he moved to the wall, eyes peering into the darkness. He could see only vague shapes in the gloom below, shadowed figures whirling in a chaotic dance as the tumult of battle continued, Sollis recognising the screams now. *Rock apes!*

He spied a loping shadow beneath, long arms and shorter legs propelling across the ground faster than any man. Sollis drew his bow until the arrow's fletching brushed his ear, centring the vertical line of the arrowhead on the running ape. Before he could loose, a loud, snarling bark of challenge erupted to his right. He spun, seeing Verkehla reeling back from the wall, a fur-covered, dog-faced shape vaulting the battlement in pursuit. Drool flew from the ape's bared teeth and clawed hands reached

out to dig into the woman's shoulders, its massive weight bearing
her down as its jaws snapped at her throat.

CHAPTER
SEVEN

SOLLIS'S ARROW TOOK the ape just behind the head. At such close range the shaft possessed sufficient force to pierce the creature's neck all the way through. It convulsed in shock, letting out a choked, rasping howl, blood colouring the drool flowing from its mouth as it whirled to face him, too slow to avoid the sword stroke that cleaved its skull. The edge of the blade cut through flesh and bone to find the brain beneath. Sollis grunted with the effort of tugging it free before finishing the twitching animal with an expertly placed slash to open the veins in its throat.

He turned his attention to Verkehla, intending to check

her wounds, but stopped at the sight of her hard, implacable features, eyes focused on something over his shoulder. Sollis ducked and rolled clear, feeling the rush of air as a claw slashed close to his head. His roll brought him to the edge of a gap in the roof. He crouched, sword held low as he regarded the second ape. This one was larger than the first with an extensive mane of fur covering its neck and shoulders, marking it out as a full grown male, possibly a pack leader. Meeting his gaze the male ape growled, sinking lower and tensing for a lunge. In such a constricted space Sollis knew he would have only one chance of a kill and decided to improve his odds, using his free hand to reach for a throwing knife. It was then that the stones beneath his feet gave way.

He arrested his fall by clamping a hand onto the edge of a roof beam, the impact jarring the sword loose from his grip, the blade whirling away into the gloom beneath his dangling feet. Seeing the ape's gaping jaws loom above, Sollis prepared to follow his sword into the depths, finding the fall preferable to the teeth. Before he could do so the ape came to an abrupt halt, jaws slackening as it shook its head, huffing in confusion. It then went into an sudden, violent spasm, head jerking back and a scream of pain escaping its maw. Sollis saw blood seeping from its eyes, nose and mouth in thick torrents. It then seemed to collapse from within, deflating like a pierced bellows as its life blood flowed out of every orifice until it was nothing more than an immobile sack of fur and bones.

Sollis watched the tide of blood wash over the roof and the part collapsed stone above, trickling down to cover the beam he clung to with both hands. Realising his grip was about to be loosened, Sollis began to haul himself up. The bloody torrent was too thick, however, and he let out a frustrated grunt as his left hand lost purchase on the beam. It flailed in the air for a second before another hand reached down to grasp his wrist. Sollis looked up to see Verkehla's face above, pale in the dim moonlight with dark stains beneath her nose and around her eyes. It appeared she had bled aplenty too.

"You're not supposed to die yet," she told him, groaning with the effort of hauling him upwards.

THE FOUR BODIES lay in the courtyard, the features of the slain Lonak warriors marred by deep claw marks that had ripped away eyes, noses and jaws. One had clearly been overwhelmed by several attackers at once, his corpse lacking a stomach as well as a face. They had been dragged into the fortress by their fellow Lonak whilst Oskin and Smentil stood in the gate, their bows cutting down a half-dozen pursuing apes. Upon descending from the tower, Sollis had conveyed the bleeding form of Verkehla to Sister Elera's care before rushing to join his brothers. However, by then the apes had retreated into the gloom. The rest of the night passed without incident, though none of the Reach's occupants managed a moment's sleep.

"Must've been near forty of the buggers, brother," Oskin said, face grim. He turned to deliver a kick to the corpse of an ape that had made it over the walls to claw a warrior to death before falling victim to a dozen or more arrows.

Closer to fifty, Smentil signed. *Approached in silence from the north. The southerly wind meant Red Ears didn't catch their scent until they were almost on us.*

"It's a miracle they only claimed four," Oskin said. "If we hadn't had these walls to retreat behind…" He trailed off and shook his head, face tense with a reluctant conclusion. "First the snow-daggers, now this. A Dark business indeed."

Sollis turned as an angry shout came from the base of the tower. "Ouch! You vicious bitch!"

"Keep your hound walking the parapet," Sollis told Oskin, making for the tower. "See if her nose has any better luck in daylight. Smentil, take position atop the tower and keep watch. I'll join you shortly."

Inside the tower he found Elera crouched at Verkehla's side. The shaman winced continually as the sister worked a needle and suture through her skin to seal the wound in her shoulder. "She's deliberately taking too long," she groused at Sollis. "I can tell. And she tortured me with some vile concoction first."

"Corr tree oil to stop it festering," Elera murmured, apparently unperturbed as she kept her attention focused on her work. Sollis assumed this was far from the first difficult patient she had treated. "And you refused redflower to dull the pain," the sister added, tying off the last stitch with a swift, practiced flourish.

"The Mahlessa has decreed we shun Merim Her drugs," Verkehla replied, teeth gritted as Elera swabbed the completed stitches with more corr tree oil. "Lest our wits become as dull as yours."

Whilst Elera fixed a bandage over the wound Verkehla let out a slow calming breath. "How many did we lose?" she asked Sollis, slipping into Lonak.

"Four. No wounded, which is strange."

"Apes rarely leave their foes alive. There's a reason my people never hunt them."

"We estimate their numbers at fifty. My brothers killed a dozen or so…"

"There'll be more," Verkehla broke in. "And not just apes. Whatever's out there isn't done with us."

Sollis stepped closer, lowering his voice a notch. "What happened up there?" he said, flicking his eyes towards the top of the tower. "I've never seen a beast, nor a man, die like that."

"It's a very big world, brother," she told him with an empty smile. "I imagine there are methods of killing beyond even your extensive experience." She paused to cast a caustic glance around the gloomy interior of the tower. When she spoke again she switched back to Realm Tongue. "The Lonak fight in the open. Castles and sieges are foreign to us. But I imagine it's something you know a great deal about."

"I know how to defend a stronghold, if that's what you mean."

"Good." She turned and called to a group of warriors waiting near the entrance, beckoning them closer. "The Blue Cloak will show you how to prepare this place," she told them in Lonak. "You will follow his word as you follow mine."

From the set, rigid faces the warriors turned on Sollis at that moment, he found himself wondering if their desire for the Mahlessa's favour was as absolute as Verkehla claimed it to be. However, none of them spoke up to protest, instead continuing to stare at him in expectant if resentful silence.

Knowing any words of conciliation would be wasted Sollis nodded and started towards the courtyard. "Follow and listen well," he told them. "We have much to do."

"WON'T WORK."

The Lonak's name was Fehl-ahkim, which translated as 'man of stone', or 'builder' depending on the inflection. He was both older and taller than most of the Banished Blades, his arms thick with muscle that flexed impressively as he crossed them, eying the ruins of the gate with an expert's disdain. Before his disgrace, which apparently involved a fatal dispute with a neighbour over the ownership of a prized pony, he had been renowned for his skill in building huts and maintaining the defensive wall of his clan's stronghold.

"Rust and rot," he told Sollis, shaking his head. "Can't build with that."

"We need to close this gate," Sollis insisted.

Fehl-ahkim shot him a sour look, jaws bunching as he sighed and cast his gaze around the innards of Morvil's Reach. "There," he said, nodding at a row of roofless stone enclosures that had once been the fortress's storehouses. "Wasted stone. We could tear it down, use it to seal the portal." He moved closer to the ruins of the gate, stroking his chin in contemplation as he touched a booted toe to one of the rusted iron brackets. "Nothing around to use for mortar, but we can buttress with these. Still some strength here, despite the rust."

"Very well." Sollis unbuckled his sword belt before removing his cloak, setting them aside and starting towards the storehouses. "Then we'd best be at it."

Under Fehl-ahkim's guidance the Lonak used their knives and war clubs to chip away the old mortar binding the stones at the base of the storehouse walls. Once they were sufficiently loosened he had them fix ropes around the top of the walls to haul them down. Within a few hours they were rewarded with a decent sized pile of building materials which the builder had begun to form into a stone and iron barrier some two feet thick at the base.

"Needs to be wider at the bottom," he told Sollis. "Elst it'll topple a the first blow of a ram, or whatever other contrivance is like to be hurled at it."

The barrier had ascended to a height of three feet by the time Sollis heard the sharp, urgent call of Smentil's hunting horn from atop the tower. Looking up he saw the brother leaning over the edge of the battlement to point west before forming his hands into a series of urgent signs. Sollis couldn't make out the full meaning at this distance but the gist was clear enough: *Enemy approaching. Many.*

"Keep working," Sollis told Fehl-ahkim before gathering up his weapons and swiftly climbing the steps to the parapet of the west-facing wall. Oskin was already there, Red Ears at his side. The hound let out a low, steady growl as she gazed at the force arrayed out of bow-shot on the far side of the river. Upon first viewing Sollis would have taken the host for a three regiment strong contingent of Realm Guard, their ranks being so neatly aligned and discipline so absolute in its lack of sound or movement. But it instantly became apparent that these were not men.

"Not just apes," Sollis murmured, echoing Verkehla as his gaze tracked along the unmoving host. A long row of snow-daggers sat still as statues next to an assemblage of equally static white pelted wolves. Smaller contingents of black bears were flanked by mountain lions and lynxes.

"How…" Oskin breathed, eyes bright with both wonder and horror. "It's impossible."

Sollis heard a similar pitch of fear and mystification in the growing murmur of disquiet from the surrounding Lonak. He caught Oskin's gaze with a hard glare and the brother abruptly straightened, offering a forced grin of apology.

"Forgive me, brother," he said. "Heard whispers of the Dark all my life. It's a strange feeling when a whisper becomes a shout."

"Quiet, you worthless goat-shaggers!" Verkehla barked, pushing her way through the throng of Banished Blades. "The Mahlessa never promised an easy path to forgiveness. So put a muzzle on that grumbling."

She came to Sollis's side, eyes narrowed as she gazed at the beasts and grunted, "Impressive," in softly spoken Realm Tongue. "It must have quite the gift."

"Who?" Sollis asked.

She pursed her lips and pointed at a solitary, two-legged figure emerging from the ranks of assembled animals. "I imagine we're about to find out."

The figure was dressed much the same as the slaughtered Kuritai they hand found back at the settlement, its cloak ripped and ragged and hair an unkempt dark mess coiling in the wind. The figure approached the western bank of the river without particular haste, coming to a halt to regard the Reach with head cocked at an angle that indicated both curiosity and amusement. After a short pause the figure bowed and opened its arms in an obvious gesture of invitation.

"A parley?" Oskin wondered.

"More likely a chance to gloat," Verkehla said, turning away with a dismissive shrug. "Ignore it. It won't attack until nightfall, and anyone who goes out there is likely to become food for its army."

"You're not curious?" Sollis asked. "Every opportunity should be taken to learn more about an enemy."

The shaman paused, rolling her eyes. "Another lesson from your years of torture at the Order House, brother?" She grinned at his annoyed frown and turned away again, waving an indifferent hand. "Go and talk with the creature if you want. I'll wager you a goatskin of wine you won't learn a thing."

HE WAS OBLIGED to clamber over Fehl-ahkim's half-finished barrier before making his way around the northern flank of the Reach to the river. As he drew closer he was able to discern more details of the figure in the ragged cloak, the most salient being that it was a woman. She watched him approach with her head still cocked at the same curious angle. Sollis detected a thin smile on her pale, hollowed features as he drew closer. He judged the woman to be of either Volarian or Realm origins from her colouring, though her starved appearance make it hard to tell for sure. However, when she spoke her accent was purely Asraelin, the inflection possessed of the sharp precision of the nobility.

"That's far enough, I think," the woman called to him once Sollis had reached the eastern bank of the river. The rushing current that separated them was loud but not so much as to muffle her voice, Sollis detecting in it a strangely juvenile note of delight. "Wouldn't want your scent to rouse my friends' baser instincts," the woman added, gesturing to the beasts at her back, all still sitting in their varied poses of statuesque immobility.

"What do you want?" Sollis asked her. He kept his hands at his sides, empty but close enough to his throwing knives for a rapid draw should he need it. He also wore his sword but had chosen to leave his bow behind. Should this parley turn ugly he would do his best to kill this woman then turn and sprint for the Reach under cover of his brothers' bows and the Lonak archers on the wall.

"I'd guess that Lonak bitch has already told you what I want," the woman said, the muscles in her emaciated face thrown into stark relief as her smile broadened. "The children you have in there," she went on, pointing at the Reach. "Give them to me."

"No," Sollis stated, voice hard and flat. He watched the woman's smile twist into a muffled laugh, eyes twinkling with what Sollis took for joyful anticipation.

"Of course you wouldn't," she said. "Even though it will certainly avail you nothing but an ugly death." She barked out a laugh, harsh and grating. "I do enjoy these rare occasions when I find one of your stripe. So desperate for the glory of self-sacrifice. So in love with the myth of their own heroism. It's always such a blissful moment when I look into their eyes at the end, watching their illusions fade, watching them cry and plead like any other dying and tormented wretch. Wouldn't you rather avoid that, brother? Give me the children and you can go back to your life of pretended courage and empty invocations to the spirits of the dead who, I assure you, are quite deaf to your entreaties."

Sollis met the woman's gaze, watching her mirth subside into an unwavering stare of deep contempt. Sollis could see a redness to her eyes now, also a thin trickle of blood coming from her nose, calling to mind Verkehla's visage the night before. The temptation to reach for his knives was strong. The distance made it a difficult throw but he was confident he could get at least one blade into her before he had to run. *Every opportunity should be taken to learn more about an enemy,* he reminded himself, suppressing the impulse.

"You have a name?" he asked instead.

"I used to," the woman replied with a shrug. "I stopped bothering to remember it a long time ago. Instead of a name, I have a purpose."

"And what is that?"

"It changes according to the place and the time. Once I warned a wealthy merchant of the necessity of poisoning his brother. Once I whispered to a queen of the treachery that surrounded her so that her court might run red with the blood of her nobles. I have persuaded generals to doom their armies and priests to damn their supplicants. And today, brother, I tell you, clearly and honestly, to hand over the children or you and everyone cowering in that pile of stones will die as slow and agonising a death as I can orchestrate. And…" She paused, tongue licking over her lips before parting to reveal teeth stained both red and yellow. "I'll reserve the worst torments for the flaxen-haired sister. Have you ever tortured a beautiful woman, brother? It's a truly addictive experience, I must say."

Don't! Sollis commanded himself, rage sending a spasm

through his hands. *Every word she speaks is valuable.* "Why?" he demanded, allowing his anger to colour his tone. "What do you want of these children?"

"Oh, isn't it obvious?" The woman arched her eyebrows in mock surprise. "I want to take them far away from these barbarous mountain savages so they can be raised in a fine palace and enjoy a life of peace and comfort for all their days."

The suddenness with which all vestige of humour slipped from her face and bearing was shocking, as if a veil had been ripped away to reveal a blank, expressionless edifice, almost as still as the beasts she commanded. "Enough talk," she said, voice different now, deeper and richer in authority. Also her accent had changed; the noble inflection replaced by something that spoke of a far distant land. Sollis would have taken it for a Volarian accent but for the discordant notes that coloured every word, almost as if two tongues were speaking at once. "Give me what I want," she said, "or I promise you I will carry out every threat spoken here."

"I doubt that," Sollis replied. "Elst why call for a parley? If your powers are so great why not just come and get them? Or is there something in there that you fear?"

The woman's eyes flicked to the Reach for an instant before snapping back to Sollis. The cadaverous face took on a decided twitch, a snarl repeatedly forming and fading from the bleached and cracked lips. Sollis wondered if she were simply mad and lost for words, but knew whatever afflicted this woman went far beyond simple lunacy.

Deciding he had learned all he was going to, Sollis turned away and started back towards the Reach. "Besides," he said.

"I'm reliably informed that I'm not supposed to die here."

"Prophecy?!" The word was spoken in a shrill, almost shrieking tone. Sollis kept walking, maintaining a steady gate, refusing to turn. "It's a lie, you pitiful dullard!" the woman screamed after him, the voice almost childlike in its rage and frustration. "Know well that whatever that bitch has told you is a lie! You *will* die here, brother!"

Sollis fixed his gaze on the Reach, taking a crumb of comfort from the sight of his brothers on the wall, flanked on either side by the Banished Blades, each bow notched and ready. The woman continued to rant as he walked, her varied threats descending into a scarcely comprehensible babble.

"I'll make you watch… when I rip the sister from nethers to neck… I'll fucking make you watch - "

Then silence. Sollis came to a halt as the woman's dissonant diatribe choked off, leaving only the faint groan of the mountain winds. Looking up, he saw his brothers and the Lonak lowering their bows as they exchanged baffled glances. When he turned he found himself regarding an empty river bank and he caught just a faint shadowy blur as the last of the beasts crested a hilltop and disappeared from view.

"You must have been awful persuasive, brother," Oskin called down to him, his voice coloured by an uncertain note of optimism.

"No," Sollis said, resuming his walk. "I wasn't."

EIGHT

THE GATE WAS sealed a good few hours before nightfall. Under Fehl-ahkim's direction the stones were piled high enough so that only a gap of a few inches remained at the top. He then used five iron buttresses to secure the barrier in place, employing bolts scavenged from the ruined original gate to affix the rusted brackets to the wall on either side.

"Will it hold?" Verkehla asked, regarding the construction with a dubious eye.

"Against charging beasts, yes," the builder replied. Sollis noted how he kept his tone carefully neutral, betraying neither respect nor disdain, though the latter shone in his eyes clearly enough.

"It had better," she told him with an empty smile. "You can stay here all night to make sure. If it falls, then so do you." She flicked a hand at a trio of Lonak warriors nearby. "You lot, stay with him."

"I'm more concerned about the walls than the gate," Sollis said quietly as they ascended to the parapet. "You saw how the apes had little difficulty in climbing all the way to the top of the tower, in silence too. They're likely to ignore the gate and simply scale the walls, overwhelm us with weight of numbers."

"I trust you're about to suggest a solution, brother," Verkehla said.

"Fire," Sollis replied. "Light torches all along the walls and cast flaming fascines over when the attack starts. If we can see them as they charge, our arrows will cut them down before they can climb up."

"I've seen a full grown ape take six arrows before it deigned to even slow its charge. And there are more than just apes among them. The Varnish have perhaps twenty arrows each. They won't last long if that thing sends all of its creatures against us at once."

Hearing a small polite cough they turned to find Sister Elera standing nearby. "I may have something that could help," she said, proffering a porcelain jar about the size of an apple.

"What is that?" Sollis asked, stepping closer as Elera removed the jar's lid. The contents appeared to be a green paste that gave off a faintly floral aroma as Sollis leaned closer to sniff it.

"Best if you don't, brother," Elera cautioned, drawing the jar back a little. "It's a mixture of nightshade and yellow-cap mushrooms, with a few other ingredients to increase the potency. I came up with it by accident last year when I was attempting to concoct a new medicine to calm a fevered heart. Instead, I produced something my novice students have taken to calling Black Eye."

"Black Eye?" Verkehla said, lips curled in suspicion as she peered at the substance.

"It has a curious effect when imbibed," Elera explained. "The white of the eye turns dark, not quite black in truth but my students tend to be overly dramatic, as the young often are."

"It's a poison," Sollis said.

"Yes. Just a small amount is sufficient to kill a grown man in seconds. I imagine a larger dose will certainly kill one of those apes, even a bear."

"Why is a Sister of the Fifth Order carrying around a jar of poison?" Verkehla enquired.

"Members of my Order often give the appearance of being defenceless," Elera replied. "It doesn't mean we are."

"Is this all you have?" Sollis asked to which Elera nodded.

"Will it be enough?" Verkehla asked him.

"If only a small dose is required, we should have enough to coat every arrowhead we possess."

"And what happens when we run out of arrows?"

"If the sister's gift can be used to coat an arrowhead it can also coat a blade. Several of your people have spears. The others will have to use their knives."

"Putting them within reach of claw and tooth."

"What battle is ever easy? Besides," Sollis met Verkehla's gaze squarely, "we have at least one other weapon within these walls, do we not?"

Her face remained impassive as she returned his stare in silence before turning and walking away, saying, "I'll have them gather in the tower so the good sister can anoint their weapons."

Sollis made sure she was out of earshot before turning back to Elera. "The book?" he asked.

She gave a somewhat sheepish wince. "Slow going I'm afraid, brother. The late Baron Morvil expended many pages on recounting his life prior to the building of the Reach. I'm compelled to the conclusion that he was either an inveterate liar or had led perhaps the most adventurous life of any soul who ever lived. I've been trying to skip ahead, find some mention of the weed but as a writer he wasn't fond of a linear narrative."

She paused to glance around before stepping closer, voice lowered. "There was one interesting passage towards the end. It's written in a hasty scrawl, so not easily read." She closed her eyes to recite from memory, "'The Wolf Men assail us from morn to moonrise. Soon it will be over. Even in my despair I know the Departed will accept me for I was wise in constructing the artery.' Later he writes his final entry, 'I have sent away those that remain. Perhaps they will find a safe route south but I will not follow. Best I die amidst this monument to my folly than suffer the shame of my father's sight.'"

"Artery?" Sollis said with a frown.

"Old Volarian often uses bodily terms when referencing architecture," she said, voice growing quieter still. "In modern Realm Tongue the closest translation is 'tunnel'."

Sollis let out a very soft laugh. "He had his builders dig an escape route."

"It would seem so."

"Where is it?"

"I have scoured this place without success, discreetly of course. The structure has no vaults, no cellars, nowhere one might expect to find such a passage. It seems his masons were skilled in concealment."

A faint flicker of movement caught the upper corner of Sollis's eye. Looking up his gaze immediately focused on a dark winged speck circling the Reach far above. The hawk was back.

"Here," he said, moving to take Elera's hand. His finger traced a shape over her open palm as she frowned at him in bemusement. "The Far Western symbol for mine or tunnel. Can you remember it?"

Her frown turned to a smile and she nodded. "He liked to mark his hiding places," she remembered.

"Quite so." He released her hand and started down to the courtyard. "I'll tell our brothers to look out for it."

"I won't leave without the children," she said, making him pause.

Sollis turned back, seeing her flexing her fingers and regarding her open hand before meeting his gaze with a steady resolve.

"Understood, sister," he said.

WHILST ELERA WENT about coating the weapons, Sollis led a dozen Banished Blades outside the walls to gather fuel for the torches and fascines. The surrounding land was rich in dense gorse bushes which he knew would take a flame and burn brightly once the leaves had been stripped from the branches.

The denuded bushes were bound into thirty or so tight bundles and soaked in the greasy reduced animal fat the Lonak used for lamp oil.

As night fell Sollis distributed the warriors evenly around the walls with orders to light the fascines and cast them into the gloom at the first indication of an attack. Smentil, being the best archer, took post in the tower. Sollis ordered Oskin to the south-facing wall with orders to make for the tower and protect Sister Elera to the end in the event of the Reach's fall. Sollis placed himself above the gate on the east-facing wall, judging it the most likely avenue of attack.

He ordered the torches lit as night descended, the orange glow banishing the gloom beyond the walls to a distance of about a dozen feet. It wasn't much of a killing ground but it would have to suffice until the fascines could be lit. Sollis had hoped the moonlight might have provided some additional illumination but the elements conspired to disappoint him. Cloud remained thick in the sky, leaving the landscape beyond the torchlight an almost blank curtain.

"What makes you think they'll attack here first?" Verkehla asked as they peered into the black.

"The slope is gentler in front of the gate," Sollis replied. "And we'd hear them if they tried to ford the river in large numbers. Besides, I had a sense our enemy is keen for this to be concluded quickly. From the looks of her, I doubt she has more than a few days of life left." He cast a sidelong glance at the shaman. "What is she? Given what we face here, it seems only fair you share what you know."

Verkehla kept her gaze averted as she provided a terse reply.

"Some things are known only to the Mahlessa."

"And yet, I suspect you still know more than you're willing to share. She's not human, is she? At least what resides within her cannot be called human."

"You see a great deal, brother."

"I see that the Mahlessa has placed us here to draw it out. The intention is for you to kill it, I suppose. With your… gift."

"If I can."

"And if you can't?"

"Then that thing will continue to ravage across these lands until it finds what it came for."

"Meaning the children we harbour here aren't what it came for."

Finally, she turned to him, a faint twinkle of amusement in her gaze. "Yes. Perhaps you can tell it that when it gets here."

"I do not appreciate being a Keschet piece in your Mahlessa's game."

"Her game is played as much for your people's protection as mine." The humour slipped from her face as she gave a derisive snort. "Always the way with your kind. For all your Faith's pretensions to wisdom, you see nothing beyond your own prejudices."

"That sounds like the voice of experience." He studied her face as it hardened further. "You lived amongst us, didn't you? That's how you know our tongue so well. Did the Mahlessa send you to learn our ways?"

"Send me?" She let out a harsh laugh. "No, she didn't send me. I was taken. Stolen from my clan when I was yet younger than the children we protect. The man who took me was a

Renfaelin knight of great renown. Having chased a war band into the mountains to no avail he and his retainers vented their wrath on a small settlement, killing all they could find, save me. He took me south to his holdfast whereupon he presented me to his wife. They had no children of their own, you see, she having lost two daughters at birth. I was to be the gift that would heal her heart."

Verkehla broke off to laugh again, the sound softer but richer in bitterness. "And I did. I resisted at first, of course. I didn't know this place or these people with their meaningless babble. Their vast huts with rooms full of pretty, shiny things that had no apparent use. Their clothes that itched and snared your feet when you tried to run. But she…"

The shaman broke off and lowered her gaze, sorrow replacing scorn as she spoke on. "She was kind, like my blood-mother in some ways, although she never beat me. And so in time my biting, screeching and smashing of crockery diminished. Their babble became words, their clothes not so uncomfortable, and I began to see meaning in the markings they scratched on parchment. For twelve years she raised me, taught me and called me daughter, though never when there were other ears to hear. They wouldn't understand, she said. I was hidden whenever visitors came calling and the master's servants promised a death by flogging if they ever spoke of my presence in his home. Then…" She ran her fingers over her forearm. "Then one day he brought home a new hunting dog. It bit me."

She fell silent, her features bunched with unwanted memory.

"You killed it," Sollis said. "With your gift."

"Don't you mean the Dark, brother?" Her eyes blazed at

him. "That's the word they spoke when they all drew away from me, terror and disgust on every face. I believe the master would have killed me then and there if she hadn't stopped him, dragged me back to the stronghold and locked me away. In the dead of night she came for me, took me to the courtyard where a horse waited. 'There is no place for you here,' said the woman who called me daughter. 'They will kill you for the Dark that infects you. You must go home.'"

"She was afraid," Sollis said. "The ability to kill with a look will stir fear in the kindest heart."

"Kill with a look." Verkehla let out an exasperated sigh, turning her gaze to the top of the battlement. "Is that what you think? See this?" She pointed to a small patch of moisture on the stone, a thimble's worth of water gleaming in the torchlight. Sollis watched as her brow creased in concentration and couldn't contain a start as the water began to alter in shape, forming a long teardrop that separated into two identical beads that blinked at him before disappearing in a cloud of vapour.

"Did you know," Verkehla asked, "that everything alive is made mostly of water? The trees, the plants, the beasts of earth and sky, you and me. We are all merely sacks of water, and it appears the Gods puts the power to command it in my hands."

She straightened, letting out a sigh rich in regret and resignation. "And so I went home. My years of comfort had made me clumsy, easily tracked once I reached the mountains. I managed to kill one of the warriors who found me before another laid me low with a club. They bound me tight and took me to the Mahlessa, as she commands be done with all those who bear a gift from the Gods. She was so old then, far older than she is now. Her body bent and twisted, but her eyes were bright with knowledge and insight. She saw all of me, all of what had been done to twist me into something that was no longer Lonak. 'You cannot be mine,' she said. 'The Merim Her have despoiled you.' And I wept. For the mother who had sent me away and the Mahlessa who now saw my worthlessness. I wept long and bitter tears until she slapped me. 'Do not whimper like them!' she said. 'Corrupted as you are, know your Mahlessa still has a use for you. The Gods would not have sent you otherwise.'"

Verkehla cast her gaze to the shrouded landscape. "And so it comes to pass. After years at the Mountain, years spent gathering this scum into the Varnish Dervakhim, years pondering the mystery of the Mahlessa's vision. Finally, I arrive here. The moment I was made for."

"Destiny is a lie," Sollis said. "Our lives are what we make of them."

"And yet here we are, brother. Just as she foretold."

Her gaze suddenly grew sharp, eyes narrowed as she peered into the gloom with predatory intensity. "It's here," she hissed. "It seems we are about to put prophecy to the test."

CHAPTER NINE

SOLLIS HAD TIME to bark out a command to light the fascines before the first beasts appeared. Four of the monstrous cats came streaking out of the gloom to throw themselves against the walls before a single arrow could be loosed. Sharp claws found easy purchase on the stone as they hauled themselves up with dismaying speed. Sollis leapt atop the battlement, drawing and lowering his bow in the same fluid movement, centring the arrowhead on the snarling maw of the cat directly below, its jaws widening in anticipation of the kill. Sollis sent his arrow into its mouth, the poison coated steel-head sinking deep. The effect was much more rapid than he expected. The cat's convulsions began almost immediately, losing its grip on the wall as it tumbled to the ground, thrashed briefly then lay still.

"It works," he heard Verkehla say with a note of surprised approval as he notched a second arrow. Pivoting to the left he sent his next shaft into the flank of another cat as it hauled itself to the top of the wall. The poison took fractionally longer to take hold this time, but the result was identical. Glancing around he saw the other two cats lying dead in front of the gate. The Banished Blades had evidently been over enthusiastic in their response for each cat had been feathered by at least a half-dozen shafts.

"Save your arrows!" Sollis called out in Lonak, repeating an order he had given several times throughout their preparations. "One for each beast is enough!"

He ordered the fascines cast over the wall. They arced out and down, bouncing along the ground until coming to rest some twenty paces out. The mingled firelight painted the landscape in shifting shades of red and gold which made the appearance of the onrushing beast horde yet more hideous. More cats came first, snow-daggers and lynxes loping up the slope in a dense mass; behind them came the pale, wraith-like wolves with the mass of apes visible to the rear.

Sollis notched again and drew a bead on the snow-dagger at the front of the pack, but before he could loose, one of Smentil's arrows arced down from the tower to take it in the haunch. Sollis altered his aim and brought down a lynx a few yards to the left. He loosed off four more arrows in quick succession, notching and releasing with a speed and automatic precision that bespoke endless hours of practice. On either side of him the

Lonak worked their bows with similar speed but less accuracy, Sollis seeing several shafts missing their mark as the horde drew ever closer. Even so, with such a wealth of targets they were less inclined to waste their arrows. Once the beasts covered the distance to the Reach it was impossible to miss and soon the ground beneath the wall became littered with the twitching corpses of cats and wolves. But many still lived, and more kept charging out of the darkness beyond the blazing fascines.

Seeing a number of wolves leap up to latch onto the wall, Sollis sank an arrow into the mass of animals below before setting aside his bow and drawing his sword. He sprinted to intercept the first wolf, the poison coated blade lancing out to skewer the beast's foreleg as it crested the battlement. It let out a strange guttural sigh as the toxin flooded its veins, Sollis seeing the truth in its name in the dark grey mist that crept into the animal's eyes at the instant of death. A pained shout drew his gaze to the right where a Lonak warrior reeled back from the wall, a trio of deep cuts on his arm. The ape that had wounded him leapt over the battlement in pursuit, claws outstretched as it sought to finish its victim, then fell dead as another Lonak sank her spear into its chest.

A quick scan of the wall revealed no more enemies for the moment, though the rising tumult of alarm from the battlement atop the gate indicated their troubles were far from over. "The bears," Verkehla said as he moved to join her, her eyes grim. Switching his gaze to the slope Sollis saw the bulk of the horde had drawn back to the fringes of the light cast by the fascines, the intervening ground blanketed in corpses. For a few seconds a curious silence settled over the scene, soon broken by the loud huffing of several large animals at the run.

Eight black bears emerged from the darkness in a tight knot, the air misted by their breath as they loped forward, a dense mass of flesh aimed straight at the gate. Sollis quickly retrieved his bow and sent an arrow into the shoulder of the leading bear. Unlike the other beasts it kept on, its loping gait slowed but not halted by the poison raging through its body. Sollis swallowed a curse and loosed again, aiming for the join between the beast's neck and torso, reasoning it to be the most likely spot for the tainted arrowhead to find a vein. The bear stumbled, back arched in pain as it let out a long final breath before collapsing to a halt.

At Verkehla's command the Banished Blades let fly with a hail of arrows, claiming another three bears. The remaining four kept on, closing the final few yards to the newly crafted barrier and throwing themselves against it with a collective roar of rage. Sollis moved back to glance down into the courtyard, seeing Fehl-ahkim and his three companions pressing their weight against the barrier as it shuddered under the impact. It was clear from the despairing expression on the builder's face that it wouldn't hold for long.

Sollis notched another arrow, one of only four remaining, and leapt up onto the battlement once more. He leaned out to draw a bead on the bears, finding they had all reared up onto their hind legs, meaning their bulk was mostly concealed by the lip of the gate's arch. He contented himself by sinking his arrow into an exposed paw then turned back, calling out to the nearest Lonak warrior, "I need a rope!"

"It's all right, brother," Verkehla said, hauling herself up to stand at his side. He stared in bafflement at the hand she held out to him. "Hold me," she said, reaching out to catch his hand in a firm grip. "I need to see them."

With that she placed her feet on the edge of the battlement and leaned out at a low angle, Sollis taking a firm hold with both hands as she focused her gaze on the bears. They had reared back a little to lunge at the barrier once more, but the assault never came. Sollis heard a low, keening groan escape the throat of one, then all, forming a kind of ghastly chorus of pain and confusion that soon choked off into a wet gargle. Glancing down he saw one stumble away from the gate to collapse a few feet away. It seemed to shrivel as it fell, the surrounding earth darkening with the fluids that leaked from every orifice. The others soon joined it in death, each one slumping down to cough out torrents of thick, dark gore until they were rendered into just a large pile of empty fur stretched over denuded bone.

Verkehla sagged and went limp, her feet slipping from the edge of the battlement. Sollis quickly hauled her back onto the parapet, drawing up short at the sight of her face. From her eyes down it had transformed into a red mask, blood flowing freely from her nose, eyes and mouth. "It's done," Sollis told her, placing a soothing hand on her forehead and finding it shockingly cold. "They're gone."

Verkehla's eyes fluttered and a faint smile played over her lips as the blood flow slowed to a trickle then stopped. "Told you…" she murmured, causing a red bubble to swell and burst on her lips. "All… just water…"

"WILL SHE LIVE?"

Elera seemed reluctant to provide an immediate answer, spending several seconds pressing her fingers to Verkehla's wrist before frowning in consternation and crouching to put an ear to her chest. "Her heart still beats," she said. "But barely." She straightened, bafflement on her face as she surveyed the unconscious woman. "This I have never seen before, brother. In truth, I don't know if there's any treatment I can offer."

"There must be something," Sollis insisted. "Some kind of medicine."

"I have stimulants that can rouse someone from a coma, if that's what this is. But she's lost so much blood, it's more likely to strain her heart yet further. I won't risk it."

Sollis stepped closer, lowering his voice. "Without her… ability, this place won't survive another attack."

"Then I suggest you find a way. I am a healer, I leave the killing to you."

Sollis drew back at the harshness of her tone, seeing the determined anger in her glare. "Forgive me, sister," he said.

Elera's ire faded into a scowl and she inclined her head in acknowledgement before turning back to Verkehla. "I suspect this state is due to her losing so much blood," she said, taking a cloth from a bowl of water and using it to wipe the drying blood from the woman's face. "It will take time for her body to make good the loss. I'll do my best to get water into her, it may help the process."

"And the matter we discussed earlier?"

She gave him a cautious glance and shook her head. "No sign of it, though I've been busy stitching wounds these past hours."

Sollis looked around at the dozen wounded Lonak in the keep, most nursing various gashes to the face and limbs. After the failed assault on the gate their enemy had tried another tactic, sending a pack of apes against the south-facing wall whilst a combined force of wolves and cats circled round to attack from the west. Fortunately, Smentil had been quick to spot the manoeuvre and Sollis had time to shift sufficient forces to contain it. Even so, the apes had managed to gain the parapet for a time, killing four Banished Blades before Oskin led a counter charge. Red Ears had been in the thick of the fighting, as evidenced by the red stain that covered her snout as she huddled beside a nearby fire. Oskin sat idly stroking her fur as he stared into the flames.

"Quite the old set-to, eh, brother?" he said with a smile as Sollis approached. "Can't remember one quite like it since the Outlaws Revolt, and that was over a decade ago. 'Course we were fighting men then. Beggared, soulless wretches the lot of them, but still men."

"You should get some rest, brother," Sollis said, sinking to his haunches and extending his hands to the fire. Now the frenzy of battle had faded the mountain chill had returned with a vengeance. He had noticed before how sensations seemed to heighten in the aftermath of combat, as if the body was reminding itself it was still alive.

"Reckon I'll get all the rest I need soon enough," Oskin replied with the faintest of chuckles.

Sollis saw it then, the paleness of his skin against the dark mask of his beard, the damp brightness to his eyes. Sollis's gaze tracked lower, seeing how his brother held his left arm tight against his chest. Reaching out he pulled Oskin's cloak aside to reveal the ragged tear in his jerkin and the bloody bandage beneath.

"I'll get our sister," he said, starting to rise.

"Leave her be," Oskin said. The soft but firm insistence in his tone made Sollis pause. He met Oskin's gaze, finding a need there, a plea for understanding. "I know a mortal wound when I see one," Oskin continued. "Big bastard of an ape caught me a good one. Took his head off for it right enough, but not before he left one of his claws inside. Too deep to be dug out. Can feel it moving about." Oskin winced, features tensing in pain. Sollis reached forward, grasping his brother's shoulder to stop him slumping into the flames. Red Ears let out a high pitched whine and nuzzled closer to her master, tail moving with frantic energy.

"Good pup," Oskin said, running a trembling hand over the hound's head. "Best I ever reared. You'll take care of her, won't you, brother?"

"I will," Sollis said. Feeling Oskin sag further he reached out to grasp both his shoulders, gently easing him onto his back.

"Dying amongst the Lonak," Oskin murmured with a bitter sigh. "My reward for a lifetime in the Order. Perhaps it's punishment for hating them so. Hate is not of the Faith after a-"

He jerked in Sollis's grip, letting out a pained shout that echoed through the keep, drawing Elera to his side. "You old fool," she said, seeing his bandage. It was soaked through with blood now, torrents of it streaming down his side. "Why didn't you come to me?"

"Leave it," Sollis said as she crouched lower to inspect the wound. "Please, sister."

She drew back, briefly meeting his gaze before looking away. "I have something that will ease his pain," she said, rising and moving to one of her saddlebags.

"Sollis," Oskin whispered, beckoning him closer. "The sign... the mark you spoke of..." His voice diminished to a croak as Sollis leaned down to put his ear to his lips. "The stables... third stall from the gate..." He fell silent, his breath playing over Sollis's cheek. Once, twice, then no more.

"Redflower with powdered green hops," Elera said, returning with a bottle in hand. "I've never met the ache it couldn't banish..." She stopped upon seeing Sollis removing the medallion of the Blind Warrior from about Oskin's neck. As Sollis pulled Oskin's cloak over his face Red Ears' whines became a plaintive howl that filled the keep, drawing the Lonak closer.

"You burn your dead, do you not?" Fehl-ahkim asked, taking in the sight of Oskin's lifeless form.

"We can't spare the fuel," Sollis said.

"Dawn is fast approaching." The builder jerked his head at his fellows who duly came forward to gather up Oskin's body. "A man who fights beside you deserves respect in death. Blue Cloak or no."

THEY PILED WHAT wood they could gather in the centre of the courtyard, a few shards from the old ruined gate and the brush wood left over from fashioning the fascines. Oskin's corpse was set atop it after which the Lonak used their scant supplies of lamp oil to douse the pyre. A warrior had relieved Smentil from his vigil atop the tower and he made his testament whilst Sollis lit the torch.

This man was my brother in the Faith, Smentil signed. *And my friend in life. Never did he falter in either regard.* He lowered his hands, turning to Sollis with an expectant nod.

Sollis chose to speak in Lonak, feeling the assembled Banished Blades deserved the courtesy for the consideration they had shown. "This man was my brother," he began. "And he taught me many things. He taught me how to follow a track across bare stone. How to read the song of the wind in the mountains. How to trust the nose of a well-bred hound. But he saved his best lesson for his dying breath: it is no good thing to die in regret, despairing of the hatred you nurtured in life."

Despite their willingness to respect Merim Her customs Sollis still saw little sign that his words engendered any additional regard amongst the Lonak. Rather, they all continued to exhibit only a stern, grudging respect. Smothering a sigh he touched the torch to the pyre, retreating a few steps as the flames took hold. They quickly enveloped Oskin's body, drawing another piteous howl from Red Ears. The hound sank to her belly and tried to crawl towards the blaze, stopping as Elera crouched to run soothing hands over her pelt.

"I know you came here to honour the word from the Mountain," Sollis went on, turning to address the Lonak. "But if the beasts come against us again in the same numbers, this place cannot be held." He exchanged a brief glance with Elera before continuing. "There is a way out, a tunnel. We can escape."

The Banished Blades shifted a little at his words, but their expressions grew puzzled rather than hopeful.

"The Mahlessa's vision is not yet complete," one said, a

stocky woman with a stitched gash on her forehead. "We will not be granted restitution until it is."

Her words heralded a general murmur of agreement from the others, Sollis seeing a certain scornful disdain on several faces. He had thought that, with their shaman laid low, their commitment to this hopeless enterprise might have waned. However, it was clear they didn't need Verkehla to sustain their obedience. The Word of the Mountain was not to be questioned.

"My brother died in your defence," Sollis said, suddenly angered by their subservience to a woman they had never seen. A woman he had sometimes suspected might be some mythical creation of their shamans, an immortal illusion designed to keep them cowering to their non-existent gods. "If you all die here his sacrifice means nothing."

"It means a man who was our enemy helped us regain our honour," Fehl-ahkim replied. "It means that our clans will speak our names once more and our stories will be shared at the fire without reproach or shame." He extended a hand to the barrier he had built, gesturing to what lay beyond. "The thing that commands these beasts is not yet slain. Flee like a worthless dog if you must, blue cloak. We are the Varnish Dervakhim, soon to be redeemed in the eyes of the Gods. We stay here."

Sollis searched his mind for some argument to sway them, but knew it to be in vain. Which left him a choice: stay and die, after having been forced to watch the woman fulfil her dire promises, or find the tunnel and leave with Smentil and Elera… and the children.

"No," Fehl-ahkim stated with emphatic resolve when Sollis raised the question. "They stay with us. The creature comes for them. They stay."

"They are innocents!" Sollis exploded, advancing on the builder, his hand going to his sword. "They do not deserve to be doomed by your Mahlessa's bloody game."

Smentil came to his side whilst Red Ears turned from Oskin's pyre to join them in facing the Banished Blades, a low growl rising in her throat. Fehl-ahkim crossed his arms, whilst the Lonak at his back tensed in anticipation of combat.

"They are innocents, yes," the builder said. "But they are Lonakhim and have learned from birth to honour the word of the Mountain. If you fight us you will die and they will stay."

Sollis's hand tensed on his sword hilt. He had no doubt the Lonak was right. There were too many for him, his brother and a grieving hound to defeat. Even so, he found his anger building. Rage was a rare emotion for him. The frequent irritations of life in the Order and the excitements of combat were one thing, but rage was another. It was something he thought he had surrendered to the masters' canes in the Order House. Now he found it sparked anew. It was the children, he knew that. Their plight stirred long buried memories of hunger and cold suffered in a dozen ruined hovels, of his mother dragging him away from one burning village after another as they fled the king's wars. Then came the day she took him to the Sixth Order mission house in a border village he still couldn't name. She held him by the shoulders, speaking in clipped, uncoloured tones that didn't reflect the rare tears shining in her eyes. *I can't feed you anymore. I spoke to the brothers. They'll take care of you now.*

He met Fehl-ahkim's eyes and drew his sword, the scrape of the blade leaving the scabbard swallowed by a pain filled scream from above. Sollis's gaze snapped to the top of the tower, finding it wreathed in some kind of dark cloud. The Lonak sentry who had taken Smentil's place writhed within it, lashing out with his war club as his screams bespoke terrible torment.

Not a cloud, Sollis realised, looking closer. *Birds.*

The birds, crows, falcons and hawks moving with an unnatural unity of purpose, whirled around the struggling warrior in an ever denser spiral until he was lost from view. They continued to mob him until he tumbled over the edge of the tower, crashing to the courtyard in a bloody spectacle of flensed skin and shattered bone. Above, the birds wheeled away from the tower before sweeping down onto the battlements below, a dark stream of flashing talons and stabbing beaks lacerating the sentries on the walls.

Sollis started for the nearest steps, intending to retrieve his bow and use what arrows remained to stem the onslaught, but skidded to a halt at the sound of something very large impacting on Fehl-Ahkim's barrier. The stone and iron construct shuddered, metal bolts squealing as they were worked loose from the walls.

"Get the children!" Sollis said, taking Elera's arm and shoving her at Smentil. "Find the tunnel."

She began to ask something but her words died as Smentil dragged her towards the keep. Sollis took a firm, two-handed grip on his sword and strode to a point some twenty paces from the gate, watching the barrier shudder again as whatever sought entry pounded at it once more.

"She found more bears," Fehl-Ahkim observed, coming to his side, war club in one hand, a knife in the other. The other Banished Blades fanned out on either side, some using their flat-bows to cast arrows at the birds still assailing their comrades on the walls, most readying their weapons as they stared at the gate in tense expectation.

"I think this might be something else," Sollis replied, seeing how the stone in the centre of the barrier had begun to bulge under the repeated battering. He was surprised to find his rage had gone now, replaced by the familiar mix of anticipation and certainty that always seemed to grip him in the moments prior to combat.

"I don't know if it's of any concern to you," he told Fehl-Ahkim. "But I'm glad I didn't have to kill you."

The builder bared his teeth as he barked out a laugh and began to reply, his words forever lost as the barrier shattered and a monster charged into the Reach.

CHAPTER TEN

THE BARRIER SHATTERED in an explosion of stone and twisted iron, Sollis and the Lonak ducking the boulders that flew across the courtyard. The four-legged beast that charged through the gate stood at least six feet tall at the shoulder, its massive, hump-backed body covered in a thick shag of black-brown fur. Its broad, bovine features were framed by a massive pair of horns, curving out into dagger-like points from a dense mass of bone in the centre of its forehead.

"Muskox!" Sollis heard one of the Lonak snarl, the stocky woman with the spear. She darted forward, nimbly diving and rolling under one of its horns to drive her spear into the beast's flank in what was evidently a long practiced move. The muskox bellowed in range and whirled, the Lonak woman leaving her spear embedded in its flesh as she dodged back, fractionally too slow to avoid the horn point that took her in the chest.

The other spear-bearing Lonak surged forward as the muskox flung the woman's body aside. It went into a frenzy of flashing hooves and scything horns, cutting down another two Lonak despite the poisoned spear blades they repeatedly jabbed into its flesh. Sollis sprinted forward and leaned back into a crouch, sliding along the mossy surface of the courtyard to slip under the muskox's belly. The star-silver edge of his sword sliced deep, unleashing a torrent of guts and blood before Sollis slid clear. He came to his feet, watching the animal let out another bellow, pain erupting from its mouth in a gout of steam as it sank to its knees. The Banished Blades fell on it, spears stabbing in a frenzy.

A fresh scream dragged Sollis's gaze to the now open gate in time to see a Lonak brought down by a trio of apes, claws and teeth biting deep whilst a tide of wolves, cats and apes rushed into the Reach. With a shout the Banished Blades charged to meet them and for a time the courtyard became a chaos of tooth, claw, knife and spear.

Sollis ducked the slashing arm of an ape then hacked it off at the elbow, the animal falling dead a second later as the Black Eye took hold. Whirling, he saw a snow-dagger coming for him, long body stretching and contracting like a spring as it closed the distance, mouth gaping. A loud, snarling growl came from Sollis's left and a brown blur caught the edge of his vision as Red Ears sprinted to intercept the cat. The hound's jaws clamped tight onto the cat's neck before they enveloped each other in a savage thrashing, tumbling away into the confusion of the courtyard.

Sollis fought down the pang of guilt as he stopped himself running in pursuit. Despite his promise to Oskin, a swift glance around the courtyard was enough to convince him there was no hope of victory now. The last of the warriors on the wall lay twitching as a crow pecked at his eyes with methodical, precise jabs of its beak. The Banished Blades still battled on in the courtyard but it seemed to Sollis that one died with every passing heartbeat. He saw Fehl-Ahkim bring down a wolf with a blow from his war club before a snow-dagger leapt on his back, its elongated fangs sinking deep into the builder's neck. Still he tried to fight on, flailing about with his club even as blood fountained from the twin wounds. Sollis lost sight of him as a quartet of wolves closed in, masking him in a mass of red and white fur.

Tearing his gaze away he ran for the stables, hacking a hawk out of the air as it swooped low to stab its talons at his eyes. He found Smentil with bow in hand, crouched behind the bulky corpse of Vensar. The stallion had plainly been set upon by multiple beasts at once, his spine clawed and bitten through in several places and his ribs showing white amidst the mass of gore that had been his chest. Sollis took a morsel of comfort from the sight of an ape lying with its skull crushed under one of Vensar's hooves.

"At least he went down fighting," he muttered, hurdling the body and crouching at Smentil's side. "The tunnel?"

His brother jerked his head to the rear then abruptly tensed and loosed an arrow. Sollis glanced back to see a charging lynx fall dead a few yards away. Proceeding into the part demolished stable, he found Elera crouched at the base of the wall, the two children and their grandfather huddled nearby. Verkehla sat slumped and grey-faced to Elera's left, Sollis seeing with surprise that her eyes were open.

"She stuffed something foul smelling up my nose," the shaman said with a grin that was more of a grimace. She flailed a hand at him. "Help me up. We need to find…"

"We're leaving," Sollis broke in. "The Reach is about to fall."

He moved to Elera's side, seeing her using a long bladed knife to scrape away the mortar surrounding a stone marked with the Far Western symbol for tunnel. Most of the mortar was already gone and Elera grunted as she worked her fingers into the gaps, vainly trying to work the stone loose.

"Won't come out," she panted. For the first time Sollis saw fear in the gaze she turned on him, though he doubted it was for her own safety. He bent lower, trying to prise the stone free but finding it stuck fast. Hearing another twang from Smentil's bowstring he tried again, grunting with the effort and cursing when the stone failed to budge.

"Could try pushing instead of pulling," Verkehla suggested in an oddly conversational tone. Her voice had the dull, distant quality of one about to lose purchase on the world.

Sollis paused then pushed a hand against the stone. At first nothing happened but then he felt it give a fraction and pushed harder. The stone slid into the wall for several inches before coming to a halt. Sollis renewed his efforts, Elera joining her weight to the labour until whatever obstructed the stone's path was either crushed or pushed aside and it slid free of their hands. Sollis heard it tumble into some empty space beyond the wall, leaving a gap no more than a foot wide.

"Not much of a tunnel, brother," Elera observed then shrank back as the lower half of the wall collapsed. The passage beyond was cramped, perhaps four feet tall, but wide enough to allow entry.

"Brother!" Sollis called to Smentil. He cast about, finding an extinguished torch that must have fallen from the parapet above, and quickly struck a flint. "Lead them on," he said, handing the lighted torch to Smentil. His brother hesitated, doubt creasing his brow until Sollis gave him a reassuring nod. "I'll be along," he said, hoisting Verkehla over his shoulder.

Smentil crouched and started into the tunnel, Elera pushing the children ahead of her as she followed close behind. Sollis nodded to Khela-hahk who took a brief look into the gloomy passage before spitting and shaking his head.

"Would you rob me of the chance for a good death, Blue Cloak?" he said. Hefting his war club, he turned towards the courtyard then paused and tugged the aged war banner from his belt. "Here," he said, tossing it to Sollis. "If the banner never falls then neither do the Stone Crushers."

The skitter of multiple claws drew his gaze back to the courtyard and he flicked an impatient hand at Sollis. "Go!"

SOLLIS HAD TO cradle Verkehla in his arms as he shuffled along the passage, his head making frequent, painful contact with the rough hewn roof. He kept his gaze fixed on the partly obscured glow of Smentil's torch, ignoring the soft but insistent protestations of the woman he carried.

"No," she groaned. "This is not her vision…"

Behind them the sound of the old man's final battle echoed

along the tunnel. The tumult continued for far longer that Sollis expected, making him wonder if the boasts of the Shatterer of Skulls hadn't been exaggerated after all. By the time the sounds of combat came to an abrupt end Sollis could see the glimmer of morning light ahead.

The tunnel opened out onto a narrow ledge barely two yards wide. It snaked along the face of a tall granite cliff rising to at least a hundred feet above. A brief glance over the edge of the cliff revealed a sheer drop into the misted depths of a canyon far below. He could see no hope of climbing either up or down, leaving them no choice but to proceed along the ledge. Smentil led the way with Elera following, the boy and girl held tight against her side. Sollis was grateful at least that dawn had finally broken, bathing the cliff face in sunlight that was for once unobscured by cloud. Navigating this route in the dark would have been impossible.

After a distance of close to a hundred paces the ledge came to an abrupt end where it met a huge curving outcrop of rock. Where the ledge joined the outcrop lay a single, steel-clad corpse. It wore the rusted armour of a Renfaelin knight, the flesh long since faded from the bones to leave a curiously clean skull. It stared up at Sollis as he came to a halt, its bared teeth conveying a distinct sense of mockery.

"At least one of Morvil's men made it out, it seems," Elera observed.

"He was wounded," Sollis said, noting the withered remnants of an arrow lying close to the fallen knight's gorget. He set Verkehla down, the shaman groaning as he propped her against the cliff.

"There must have been others," Elera went on, glancing around at the walls of granite. "Perhaps they climbed out."

Or got tired of starving and jumped, Smentil signed. He scanned the cliff above with an expert eye before turning to Sollis with a grim shake of his head. *No handholds.*

A strange groaning sound drew Sollis's gaze back to the far end of the ledge and the small dark opening of the tunnel. It took him a moment to recognise it as the massed breath of many beasts in a confined place.

"There must be some way," Elera insisted, sinking to her knees and peering over the lip of the ledge. "If they couldn't climb up, perhaps they…" She trailed off, then a moment later voiced a soft, surprised "Oh!"

"What is it?" Sollis asked, moving to crouch at her side in the hope she might have discovered some means of navigating the cliff. Instead he found her staring at a cluster of small plants growing from a patch of moss-covered rock a few feet down. Plants with narrow stems from which sprouted four, pale white flowers.

"Jaden's Weed," Elera said, voice both sad and joyful. She reached out a hand, lowering herself further over the edge.

"I think we have more pressing concerns, sister," Sollis told her, reaching out to ease her back.

Feeling an insistent pat on his shoulder he turned, finding Smentil sinking into a crouch, bow aimed at the beasts now emerging from the tunnel. The apes came first, streaming out of the hole in a dense mass at least thirty strong, spreading out to scale the cliff above and below. They seemed immune to falling, their claws making effortless purchase on the stone. The cats came next, far fewer in number but showing similar agility. Lynx and snow-daggers seemed to bound across the rock. Of the wolves Sollis could see no sign, making him wonder if they had all perished at the hands of the Banished Blades.

Smentil's bow thrummed, Sollis seeing a large male ape slip lifeless from the cliff-face, dislodging two of his companions as he tumbled into the depths. Smentil's next shaft took down a snow-dagger, his third another ape, then his string fell silent. He gave Sollis a helpless shrug, gesturing at his empty quiver before setting the bow aside and drawing his sword. Sollis followed suit, moving to stand in front of his brother and pausing to cast an urgent glare at Elera.

"Do you have any Black Eye left?" he asked.

"A little. But what good will it..?" She fell silent as he switched his gaze to the children. They sat huddled together at the end of the ledge, faces pale though lacking in tears. It occurred to Sollis that he had seen neither of them cry during this whole sorry episode.

"I don't know why she wants them," he said. "But I know it will be a kinder end."

Elera's features seemed to drain of colour and expression as she stared back at him. In anger or grim resolve he couldn't tell. "Very well," she said in a harsh whisper, reaching for her pack.

Sollis turned back to the approaching beasts, finding the nearest ape no more than ten yards off. He was reaching for a throwing knife when the beast came to a sudden, frozen halt. The stillness quickly spread to the rest of the horde. Every ape and cat stopping to hang from the rock, breath misting the air as they stared at their prey, eyes empty of either hunger or rage.

"Such perfect soldiers they make," a voice said, echoing from the tunnel mouth. The woman emerged into the light in a crouch, straightening to move along the ledge with a somewhat unsteady gait, reminding Sollis of a drunken lush seeking to convince others of her sobriety. Her features were even more emaciated now, streaked by blood that rendered them into something from a nightmare.

She bleeds like Verkehla, Sollis realised. *These gifts extract a heavy price it seems.*

"No grumbling, no lust for loot or rapine," the woman continued as she approached. "No wayward thoughts or dreams of past lives to trouble my hold on them." She came to a halt twenty yards away. Too far for an accurate knife throw. "Would that it was always so easy."

She angled her head to survey them, baring reddened teeth in an awful smile as her gaze alighted on the children. Sollis saw her lips twitch in anticipation when her eyes tracked to Verkehla.

"Not yet dead," she said with a wistful sigh. "I thought I felt a spark still fluttering away."

To Sollis's surprise Verkehla let out a harsh, half-choked laugh. "Such a fool," she said, shaking her head as she climbed to her feet. She sagged against the stone and Smentil reached out to help her up, drawing a faint smile of gratitude. She leaned heavily against the cliff as she moved to Sollis's side, her voice dropping to a murmur. "Baroness Yanna Forvil," she said. "You'll find her in a holdfast near the north Renfaelin coast. If she still lives, I should like her to know I never blamed her, never hated her for what she did."

Sollis reached out to steady her as she swayed but she

shook her head, face drawn in pain as she clawed her way along the ledge to confront the woman. "The wolf already took what you came for," she told her. Sollis took note of how she leaned against the cliff, both hands flat against the stone. "The child is far beyond your reach now."

The grin disappeared from the woman's face as her gaze, fiercely inquisitive now, switched back to the children.

"Just bait," Verkehla told her, laughing again. "And how willingly you stuck your leg into the snare. All the years you have infested this world, and still you retain no more wit than the beasts you command."

The woman let out a snarl every bit as bestial as anything uttered by one of her beasts. The horde instantly resumed its charge, apes and cats swarming across the stone.

"Water," Sollis heard Verkehla say and saw that she was smiling at him, fresh blood streaming from her nose and eyes. "It's in everything, brother. The air, the earth, even the mountains…"

He felt it then, a deep tremble in the stone beneath his boots. "Back!" he told Smentil, pushing his brother towards the far end of the ledge. A huge, thunderous crack sounded and he whirled, seeing a fissure open in the cliff where Verkehla had placed her hands. Fragments of stone flew as the crack extended along the length of the cliff, sending several beasts tumbling into the canyon. He saw the woman charging along the ledge, a short sword in her hand and murderous intent on her wasted features as she closed on Verkehla.

The torrent exploded from the fissure like an axe blade, snatching away the woman and Verkehla with a swift, savage blow. They hurtled into the depths of the canyon, Sollis hearing a final scream of enraged frustration from the woman, but not a sound from the shaman. The water gave a monstrous roar as it continued to pour from the fissure, more cracks snaking through the stone to unleash fresh torrents, sweeping the entire beast horde away in a scant few seconds. It abated after several minutes of fury, leaving them gaping at a misted cliff face shot through with a rainbow as the sun crested the eastern ridge.

Of the beasts only one remained, an ape perched high above the fissure and staring about in obvious terror and confusion. It let out a plaintive hoot as its eyes roamed the canyon, no doubt searching for vanished pack-mates. Its calls subsided when no answers came and Sollis saw it cast a curious glance in his direction before it climbed to the top of the cliff and hopped from view.

Sollis rose from the tight crouch he had adopted, looking down to check on the others. Smentil stared about in relieved amazement, as did the children. Elera's face, however, betrayed no joy at their deliverance. Instead, clutching her jar of Black Eye with such a depth of shame and guilt on her face that Sollis found it hard to look upon.

"You didn't…" he began, moving to the children, staring into their eyes for the encroaching grey mist.

"No," Elera said, voice soft with self-reproach. "I couldn't. I… I am a coward, brother."

"Nonsense." Sollis bent to grasp her elbow, helping her up. "There were no cowards here. Now, let's see about retrieving your weed."

CHAPTER

ELEVEN

▮ deluge and they made an untroubled journey back to the tunnel and into the Reach. The fortress was littered with the corpses of the Banished Blades and the dozens of beasts they had slain. Of all the souls that had fought in defence of this place only one remained alive.

Red Ears sat atop the corpse of the snow-dagger she had killed, letting out a soft huff of welcome as Sollis approached to rub a hand over her bloody snout. Her pelt bore numerous scars but nothing he fancied would leave lasting injury. He glanced up at a touch from Smentil, finding him pointing to a trio of Lonak ponies near the west-facing wall. Having somehow survived the carnage, they stood shivering in distress but otherwise unharmed.

At least we won't be walking home, Smentil signed.

NIGHT WAS FALLING when they drew within a mile of the Lonak settlement. Torches blazed all along on the defensive wall, indicating a continued sense of insecurity amongst the inhabitants. The torches also convinced Sollis it would be highly unwise to venture any closer.

"Are you sure they'll take them in?" Elera asked as Sollis lifted the children from the back of her pony.

"It's a Grey Hawk settlement," he said. "No clan ever turns away its own blood."

"But without parents who will care for them?"

"All Lonak are parents to the children of their clan. Their ways are not ours, sister."

"My Order has many orphanages. Places where they will be cared for, educated…"

"Also shunned and hated."

Sollis sank to his haunches in front of the children, taking the Lonak war banner from where it hung on his belt and holding it out to the boy. "If the banner never falls, neither do the Stone Crushers," he said in Lonak.

The boy looked briefly at the banner before pushing it away. "He wasn't really our blood-grandfather," he said. "Just a braggart with no living kin. He only claimed us so the Varnish wouldn't kill him for his cowardice."

He cast a scowling glare at each of them in turn, small mouth twisting as he spoke the words, "Merim Her!" The boy spat on the ground before taking hold of his sister's hand and dragging her towards the settlement. The girl looked back only once at Elera, a very small smile of what might have been gratitude on her face. Then they were lost to the gloom, two small shadows hurrying towards refuge.

SOLLIS FOLLOWED AS short a route as possible to the pass. He didn't know if they still enjoyed the Mahlessa's protection and was keen to escape the mountains before word spread amongst the clans that the Grey Eyed Fox now travelled their dominion virtually unprotected.

They reached the pass after three days hard riding, dismounting in front of the outer gate and setting the ponies loose. Once inside Sollis and Elera gave a fulsome account of their mission to Brother Commander Arlyn who listened in silence throughout. Sollis had expected some questions or even doubt when they came to describe what had undoubtedly been use of the Dark, but Arlyn's reaction had been only a half-raised eyebrow. When they were done he nodded, offering one of his meagre smiles.

"My thanks to you, brother and sister," he said. "Your report is duly noted."

Sollis found himself blinking in surprise. "The woman, brother," he said. "It was clear to me she acted as part of a larger design. We must warn the other Orders, pass word to the king…"

"As I said, brother," Arlyn broke in, his voice possessed of an uncharacteristically hard tone within which lay a clear command to silence. "Your report has been noted."

Arlyn used a long-fingered hand to lift a length of inscribed parchment from his desk, his tone softening to genuine sorrow. "Sadly, it seems I have grim news to share."

"The Red Hand?" Elera said. "Has it spread?"

"Not to my knowledge," Arlyn replied. "This pertains to another matter. Aspect Andril has succumbed to age and illness. Our senior brothers have called me to the Conclave. They wish me to submit myself for confirmation as Aspect of the Sixth Order."

"There can be no better choice," Sollis said.

Arlyn gave a slight incline of his head. "We shall see. It is ultimately for the Conclave to decide. In one week I shall return to Varinshold. During my absence you will be Brother Commander of the Skellan Pass."

"As you wish, brother."

"As to your remarkable story," Arlyn went on, rising and moving to the narrow window behind his desk. "My many years in service to the Faith have left me of the opinion that such things are best left to the shadows. There will be no written account of your journey and I require that you speak no word of it to another soul without my explicit command."

He only gave a vague nod as Sollis and Elera spoke their agreement, the corners of his thin-lipped mouth turning up a little as he gazed out at the walls of the pass. "I believe I might actually miss this place."

"YOU'RE SURE YOU'LL be able to find it?"

"The holdfast of Baron Forvil near the north Renfaelin coast." Elera tightened a strap on her mount's saddle, one of the more placid Order mounts from the stables. "I doubt it will be hard to locate, brother."

"Thank you. I would go myself but…"

"The Faith requires that you stay here and fulfil your duties. I know." She ran a hand over her saddle bags, frowning. "Brother

Oskin gave his life for a weed. A cure to a disease that may never trouble this Realm again."

"It will ease his soul in the Beyond to know that at least now we can defend against it should we need to."

"It could take years to develop a cure, and perhaps sharper minds than my own. But yes, at least now we have a chance." She turned to him, her frown deepening to sad reflection. "A battle fought. Great courage shown. All those people lost. And the tale will never be told."

"The Lonak will tell it," he assured her. "When the night grows dark and they gather at their fires. They will speak of the Varnish Dervakhim who redeemed themselves in the eyes of the gods. And the shaman who led them and died to honour the word from the Mountain."

"And us? Do you think they'll speak of us?"

"They will." Sollis thought of the Lonak boy's final, sneering farewell. "But not well."

She laughed a little, but sobered quickly. "What was it? That *thing*?"

"I wish I had some notion, sister. Perhaps it was something that defies our understanding. But I doubt this world has seen the last of it."

She reached out to clasp his hand, her grip strong with certainty. "Something stirs, brother," she said. "Something Dark and terrible. We will be needed. All other needs, or wants, must be set aside."

She met his gaze for a brief second, her eyes a brighter shade of blue than he had seen before, and Sollis realised they were close to tears.

"Oh well," she said before he could respond. She released his hand and turned to climb into the saddle. "Best be off. Be sure to say goodbye to Brother Smentil for me, and your dog, of course."

With that she spurred her mount to a trot and rode through the southern gate. Although he tried to resist the impulse, Sollis found himself climbing the steps to the battlement. Looking to the south he spied a small grey figure amidst the heather clad slopes, riding with practised ease, keeping her gaze firmly on the trail ahead. Somehow, in a small, rarely explored corner of his heart, Sollis knew she badly wanted to turn around as much as he wanted to go after her.

ABOUT THE
AUTHOR

Anthony Ryan was born in Scotland in 1970. After a long Career in the UK Civil Service he took up writing full time after the success of his first novel *Blood Song*. His books have been published by Ace/Roc, Orbit, and Subterranean Press. Anthony's work has also been published internationally, being translated into sixteen languages.

For more information on Anthony's books visit his website at: anthonyryan.net.

Follow Anthony on:

Twitter: @writer_anthony

Facebook: www.facebook.com/anthonyryanauthor

Instagram: anthonyryan286